TAKE ME NOW

LIGHT MY FIRE SERIES

J.H. CROIX

To Erin - you make me look like something other than a hot mess. Thank you for your kindness, patience and detail-wizardry.

Sign up for my newsletter for information on new releases & get a FREE copy of one of my books!

http://jhcroixauthor.com/subscribe/

Follow me!

jhcroix@jhcroix.com
https://amazon.com/author/jhcroix
https://www.bookbub.com/authors/j-h-croix
https://www.facebook.com/jhcroix
https://www.instagram.com/jhcroix/

Chapter One

FARRAH

I hurried to the front of the vet clinic, practically skidding through the door into the reception area. Our office manager and ruler of our vet clinic universe was out today. That left me handling my vet tech duties and fumbling through managing the reception area as well.

My shoes squeaked on the tiled floor as I came to a stop just as my eyes collided with who had to be the sexiest man I'd ever seen. He was holding a cat carrier and peering inside it.

"Hi, can I help you?" I asked, my voice sounding a little breathless.

The man glanced up, and my hormones clambered up to take a thorough look. He had dark hair with a wave that curled along his collar paired with cognac eyes. He was dressed simply in a T-shirt with a battered denim jacket thrown over it. The jacket hung open, revealing the muscled planes of his chest. The T-shirt did little to disguise them. He had broad shoulders and easily cleared six feet tall, based on my guess.

"I'm here. With Humpty. He has an appointment." He pointed at the cat.

I glanced down at the calendar. Fortunately, our office manager extraordinaire, Tiffany, had left us a paper calendar. Although Alice, my boss and the vet here, and I were savvy with the computer scheduling program, Tiffany anticipated we'd be too busy to deal with it on our own.

"You must be Cooper. Cooper Hughes?" I prompted

"That's me." His voice was low and gruff.

He held my gaze directly. I felt somehow as if this man, who I had now spent maybe two minutes with, could see right through me.

I shifted on my feet. "Great. Well, come on back."

I rounded the desk and opened the door that led into the back hallway. Humpty let out a disgruntled wail when Cooper lifted the cat carrier.

Cooper glanced toward me. "He hates being in this thing."

Cooper had a straight nose and cheekbones that angled up almost dramatically. But it was his strong jaw with clean lines that got to me.

When he smiled a little, his eyes crinkled at the corners and his mouth kicked up higher on one side. My hormones let out a noisy cheer and butterflies flitted about in my belly.

I cleared my throat, trying to stay focused. "Most cats aren't fans of cat carriers."

Cooper walked by me when I gestured him through the door. I scurried ahead in the hallway. "Right through here." I walked into one of our exam rooms.

Alice was still finishing up in an exam room farther down the hallway with another patient, an exuberantly friendly and elderly lab-mix dog. I closed the door once Cooper was in the room. "You can just set his carrier right there on the table." I pointed at the stainless-steel exam table in the center of the room.

"So what's going on with Humpty?" I asked as I stood opposite from Cooper on the other side of the table.

Humpty studied me through the bars of his carrier. He was a rather rotund orange cat.

Cooper took a breath and squared his shoulders. "He keeps scooting his butt around. Like a lot. I looked it up online, and it says he might need his anal glands expressed." He let out a sigh. "Apparently, some people do this themselves. I'm pretty sure Humpty will hate me forever if I even think about trying to do that."

I chuckled. "He probably wouldn't love it. If he's scooting around like that, it's possible we need to do that. But let's have our vet take a look. If that's the issue, we can take care of it today. I can show you how to do it if you'd like." When Cooper's brows hitched up skeptically, I grinned. "Or you might decide to bring him to us regularly for it."

Cooper looked at Humpty before nodding. "I'm pretty sure I'll be bringing him here." When his eyes met mine again, he shrugged, offering a sheepish grin.

"Understood. I'm a vet tech, and it's not my favorite thing to do."

Just then, there was a quick knock on the door, and Alice stepped through. She cast a smile at Cooper. "Hi, I'm Alice, the vet." She stopped in front of Humpty's cat carrier, peering inside. Humpty shifted backward slightly, eyeing her with deep suspicion. Glancing at Cooper, she added, "He looks thrilled to be here."

Cooper cracked a grin. "He's not so sure about this whole situation. I'm Cooper. This is Humpty."

"Humpty might need his anal glands expressed," I chimed in. "Apparently, he's been scooting his butt around."

"All over my apartment," Cooper added.

Alice's eyes twinkled as she lifted her hands to tighten her auburn ponytail. "Well, then, let's take a look. Do you mind if I take him out?"

"Go for it." Cooper gestured toward Humpty.

The moment Alice opened the cat carrier, Humpty barreled out, jumping off the table and leaping from the floor to the counter, where there was a sink with some cabinets above it. Cooper moved to catch him, but he zipped around the room so fast that he made it challenging. His size didn't slow him down one bit.

It was a scramble, but I managed to get ahold of Humpty and held him in my arms while he wailed in protest. Cooper grinned. "You're faster than me."

"Well, I'm used to catching cats who hate coming here."

I stepped to the side of the table, carefully placing Humpty on it, all the while keeping a firm hold on him. Several minutes later, Alice had checked him over and glanced at Cooper. "It's definitely his anal glands. Farrah can help with that. It might comfort Humpty if you stay in the room. Meanwhile, I don't know when he had his last annual appointment, but we can schedule one for him."

Cooper shrugged. "I don't know. I got him as a rescue. How about I schedule one on my way out?"

"Sounds good," Alice replied. Just then, the chime from the reception area rang out in the hallway. "I'll handle that. You've got this?" She glanced at me with her brows arched in question.

"Absolutely. Anal gland expression is my expertise," I deadpanned.

She chuckled before departing the room. That left me in there with Cooper and Humpty. Everything went to shit. Literally.

Humpty was absolutely not a fan of the process and made his displeasure known with dramatic wailing and irritated wiggling. By the time it was all said and done, I was totally flustered, and Cooper was doing his best not to laugh. I finished the job, and we got Humpty cleaned up and back in his carrier. He was so offended by the situation he wouldn't even accept a treat from me.

After I washed my hands and changed out of my lab coat, I looked over at Cooper. "Well, that could've gone better."

Cooper threw his head back with a laugh. My belly swooped.

When he leveled his gaze with mine again, he said, "I really appreciate this, and I will definitely be using you all to do this in the future."

Chapter Two

COOPER

The vet tech stood in front of me. We had just wrangled Humpty back into his cat carrier, and I could feel him looking at me. He was deeply offended by the situation. Maybe I hadn't had him that long, but he let his feelings be known.

Meanwhile, the vet tech, whose name I couldn't seem to recall, turned away to wash her hands in the sink. My eyes snagged on her blond ponytail. It curled up at the end, swinging with every motion she made. She was tall with slender shoulders. My eyes trailed along the dip at her waist and the generous flare of her hips. My greedy gaze shifted lower over the lush curve of her bottom.

I should've been grateful for the distraction Humpty offered. Yet it didn't do much good. This woman encompassed all of my focus.

She said something as she turned around, drying her hands on a paper towel. "Cooper?" she prompted.

I gave my brain a hard kick. *Focus.*

"Yeah?" I returned as if I didn't even notice she had said something before that. My awareness had heard her distantly, but I didn't know what the fuck she said.

"I was asking how long you've been in Willow Brook." She blinked, and her eyes looked even brighter and greener when her lashes lifted again. She glanced away when the door to the exam room opened.

Alice, whose name I actually remembered, looked at her. "Farrah, I was wondering if you can be out front in a few minutes? My next appointment will be here soon, and I'm running behind with this one."

Farrah? How the hell had I forgotten *that* name?

Farrah nodded. "Yep, we're just finishing up. I'll walk Cooper and Humpty out."

Alice gave me a quick smile. "Nice to meet you, Cooper." Her eyes shifted to Humpty. "You as well, Humpty." She looked back at me. "He'll get over it. I promise."

"I hope so. Thank you."

"Of course. I'll see you and Humpty when he's here for his annual checkup."

Alice left with a wave just as Farrah let out a low and throaty little laugh. Everything this woman did was like a direct hit into a vein of desire. What in the ever-loving fuck was going on with me? I wasn't in the habit of getting so sucked into a woman that I couldn't even remember her name—much less being affected by a woman's laughter.

Humpty hissed from his crate.

"Farrah isn't the most common name," I observed. "The only Farrah I can think of is Farrah Fawcett. I had a crush on her when I was in high school."

Farrah, the living and breathing one standing in front of me, snorted. "My parents named me after her."

I studied her honey-blond hair with the curl at the

end of her ponytail and her big green eyes with thick lashes. "It suits you," I offered.

Farrah's eyes twinkled. "I actually liked Farrah Fawcett. She was my personal role model and an inspiration when I was growing up."

"Oh?"

She nodded. "Mom was a fan of Farrah's when she was really popular in my mom's younger days. I always wanted to meet her. She seemed badass and beautiful. Even though she's gone, she's still an inspiration to me. I figure I might as well embrace my namesake."

I lifted Humpty's carrier and held the door as Farrah walked through, smiling up at me. Her lips were maybe a foot away from mine, and I wanted to slide my arm around her waist, pull her close, and kiss her. For God's sake, she had just "expressed" my cat's anal glands. Nothing about this moment should've been sexy.

Except *she* was sexy as all hell. She stirred up desire and muddled my thoughts just by existing near me.

"And do you think you've lived up to her?" I asked lightly, telling myself I was just making casual conversation.

"Bullshit," my skeptical, cynical mind retorted.

That side of my brain taunted, but even stronger than that was a fierce voice. That one was fucking loud. *Forget her.*

A new but far too familiar sense of bitterness rose inside. I ignored it.

I wanted to linger as we reached the door that led out to the reception area. I wanted to have this conversation. Farrah *was* badass and beautiful to me. Yet I sensed she didn't feel that way, and I wanted to know why. I wanted to know all of her secrets.

I opened the door just as she reached for the

handle, and our hands brushed. A sizzle of electricity raced up my arm, spinning into the heat that had been simmering on low burn ever since I'd looked into Farrah's eyes.

She looked up at me, her eyes widening slightly as if she had felt the same jolt of electricity. She shrugged as she took her next step, replying, "I don't know. I don't think so."

The next thing I knew, my mouth got ahead of my brain. "You're definitely beautiful." I was completely serious, my voice sounding almost earnest.

She missed a step, stumbling and catching her balance before she spun back to face me. "Oh!" Pink tinged her cheeks. Need sank its claws deeper. "Thank you," she finally said, looking so surprised I didn't even know what to think.

How the hell did she not know she was beautiful? Surely, she had men beating down her door.

"Hi, Farrah," a voice said.

Holy hell. I hadn't even noticed someone was out in the waiting area. I kicked my brain into gear. Cynical didn't even come close to capturing the man I'd become in the last year or so of my life. I hated it.

Farrah glanced over, smiling when she saw the woman who stood there.

"Cooper, nice to see you!" exclaimed Janet James, the owner of *the* favorite coffee shop in town.

I forced myself to step away from Farrah, creating what I hoped was enough distance for me to think. I dipped my chin as I smiled at Janet. "Hey there, Janet. How's it going?"

Humpty let out a disgruntled meow from his carrier as Farrah set it on the reception counter.

Janet looked at Humpty. "This must be your cat?"

Since I rented from Janet, she knew I had a cat,

but she hadn't officially met him. "Sure is. This is Humpty. He just had his anal glands expressed, and he's not happy about it. I hope he forgives me soon." I shrugged.

Janet burst out laughing. "That's why I'm here." She gestured to a cat carrier on one of the chairs. "I just got a cat from the rescue program. He's old and really affectionate, but he scoots everywhere."

Farrah laughed as she rounded the reception counter. "Let me check Cooper out and then Alice can take a look. If that's the issue for your cat as well, I can also show you how to take care of it yourself."

Janet was already shaking her head. "I'm game for many things, but not that."

I chuckled as we stepped to the reception counter together. "That's pretty much what I said."

"Remind me how you ended up with Humpty," Janet prompted.

"Wes convinced me to adopt him," I explained, referring to a friend from work. Like me, Wes was a hotshot firefighter. He also helped his mother with a local animal rescue program.

"Wes is a convincing guy," Janet agreed with a grin.

"They're never short on cats at the rescue program," Farrah chimed in as she tapped on a keyboard. "That'll be fifty dollars."

"Well worth it." I slipped my wallet out of my pocket and handed over a credit card.

"I'll pay extra," Janet chimed in. "Can it go toward the vet care you provide for the rescue program?"

"Absolutely," Farrah said.

"You can charge me double, then," I offered. "Honestly, though, you should probably be charging more for that."

Farrah shrugged as she swiped my credit card and

handed it back. "We try to keep our fees affordable, and that's pretty standard."

"Cooper is a firefighter. He must know Jonah," Janet said to Farrah.

Farrah's pretty green eyes lifted to mine. "Oh! Jonah is married to Alice, if you didn't know."

"Ah, no wonder she looks familiar. I think I met her for like a minute at Wildlands last month. We were getting together after work, and Jonah left early."

"There's no shortage of firefighters in this town, so you'll have lots of friends," Farrah offered. "Let's get Humpty scheduled for that annual exam."

A few minutes later, we had an appointment confirmed. I fought the urge to linger, but Farrah was already focused on Janet's cat.

"Good to meet you, Farrah. I'm sure I'll see you soon," I offered with a glance at Janet.

As I drove away, I told myself not to make a move on Farrah. She was clearly friends with people I knew. I didn't need any complications in my life. My crazy reaction to her could be chalked up to nothing more than the fact that she *did* strike a resemblance to my high school crush. Maybe it was odd that I had the hots for Farrah Fawcett when I was growing up, but it all started when my mom used to watch *Charlie's Angels*. She said it was her comfort show. Seriously.

As a fourteen-year-old boy, Farrah Fawcett was the most beautiful woman in the universe to me. Her image had been cemented as a fantasy for me then.

Fantasy was all the real-life Farrah I'd just encountered could ever be. I'd done the whole love and romance thing once, and that had been enough. It had blown up in my face when my fiancée fucked one of my good friends.

Chapter Three

COOPER

Just as I was starting my truck to drive home and drop Humpty off, the emergency ringer sounded on my phone. A few minutes later, I had confirmed our hotshot crew had a call to fly out to a fire within a half hour.

I had time to zip by the station before we were scheduled to leave, but I didn't have time to find someone to take care of Humpty.

That had been my primary concern when Wes persuaded me to adopt him. I had just moved into a new apartment after the short-term rental I'd been staying in was no longer available. I hadn't found someone to take care of him when I was out in the field yet.

Maybe three minutes later, I jogged into the Willow Brook Fire & Rescue Station. Maisie Steele glanced up, her brown curls bouncing around her shoulders when she turned to look at me. "Why are you coming in through the front?" As the main dispatcher for Willow Brook Fire & Rescue, Maisie handled the reception area. She was also married to a crew superintendent for a different hotshot crew here in Willow Brook, Alaska.

"I got the call we're scheduled to leave, but I'm just checking to see how much time I have before the helicopter will be here. I was just leaving a vet appointment with my cat, Humpty, the one I adopted from the rescue program," I explained.

"They're actually already here," she replied.

"Fuck." I pressed my tongue into my cheek, considering my options.

Before I could say anything more, Maisie interjected, "Don't worry about it. I can take Humpty to your place. Did you have someone who checked on him before?"

Shaking my head, I replied, "I just moved. At the place I was staying short-term, my neighbor downstairs checked on him for me."

Maisie waved a hand dismissively. "Go park in the back and bring him in to me. I'll find somebody. If anything, I can handle it."

"Are you sure?" I hesitated.

"Absolutely. Go!" She waved me toward the door. "You need to get ready to leave," she ordered.

I hustled out. A moment later, I delivered Humpty to her. Just as I was opening the door to the back hallway, Rowan Cole, one of my friends and one of the reasons I was here in Alaska, was coming through. "Oh, hey there," he said. "We've got two crews heading out. Are you going with us?"

"Headed to the locker room right now to grab my gear."

"All right, see you out back."

Rowan was from my hometown—Stolen Hearts Valley, North Carolina. He'd ended up here in Alaska to chase the thrill of hotshot firefighting like me, along with another friend from our hometown, Remy Martin. The world could be small.

I'd trained as a firefighter in North Carolina with Remy and Rowan. When Remy heard about what happened with my ex-fiancée, he told me he'd give me a shout if there was an opening out here, promising me I'd love it. I'd needed more than one reason for a change of scenery. Between my world blowing up and learning how many people had known about one of my friends having a yearlong affair with my ex-fiancée, it was safe to say that knowledge had burned a lot of bridges for me. Even worse, my dad's death before that had sent me spiraling into grief.

I'd always said I'd been blessed to have my parents. I had, but it hurt all the more to lose my dad as a result. Cindy's explanation, or her lame-ass excuse as far as I was concerned, for why she'd looked elsewhere when I caught my old friend balls deep inside her was that I hadn't been emotionally available since my dad had died.

Maybe that was true, but I guess I was one of those people who believed you should be there for each other, even when things were hard. Especially when life knocked you down.

As I quickly changed into my gear and jogged out to the helicopter, my mind spun back to Farrah and the look of surprise in her eyes when I'd pointed out the obvious truth. She *was* beautiful. I wanted to see her again, and I knew that was stupid.

I was in no shape for romance. At all.

Chapter Four

FARRAH

"Pass me that bottle of wine, please," Alice said, holding her hand up.

I handed it across the table while Maisie looked askance at her. "Rough day?" she prompted.

"Hell, yes. I had two emergency surgeries. I really need to hire another vet," Alice replied as she filled her wineglass.

As a sort of new person in town, I was still getting to know everyone, but Alice and Tiffany made sure I came along when they had occasional card nights with a group of friends in town. Many of these women had been born and raised here, while I was still assimilating into the small world of Willow Brook, Alaska.

"Who's driving?" Tiffany Mills prompted. Tiffany was our office manager and would be working to get caught up for us in the office after being out the day prior.

"I'm the designated driver," Amelia offered with a glance down at her belly. "Because I'm pregnant, and I can't drink. I hate being pregnant, but it's not because I can't drink. My back hurts all the damn time."

"Well, I'm sorry about that, but we're all grateful you're driving," I offered with a smile, lifting my wineglass and taking a swallow. Amelia chuckled. I looked at Alice. "Also, I know you had two emergency surgeries, but I swear my job title for the day was anal gland expresser. Three cats and two dogs today."

Maisie grinned. "I have one of your cats."

"I don't have a cat," I pointed out, looking her way curiously.

"Humpty. I meant one of the cats whose glands you expressed. The guys all went out to a big fire north of here yesterday. Cooper showed up with his cat because he didn't have time to find someone to check on him. I meant to ask Janet, but I forgot, so I just took Humpty home with me. I need to find someone else, though, because our cat is seriously pissed about it," she explained.

"I can take Humpty," I offered.

"Really?" At my nod, she added, "He's cute and sweet, but our cat is a ball of hissing. He also sat in the window with his back to me this morning."

Tiffany let out a laugh. "Your cat sounds passive-aggressive."

Maisie's brown curls swung as she nodded vigorously. "He totally is." Her gaze shifted to me again. "Are you serious about taking Cooper's cat while he's gone? It could be a week or more. You never know how long the crews will be out when they go to a fire."

"Sure. I met Humpty when Cooper brought him in yesterday. It was a fun appointment," I said dryly.

Lucy Phillips snorted from where she was seated beside me. "I can't imagine doing that. I'm glad all we have is a hamster."

"And, how is Ham 2?" Alice prompted as she set her wineglass on the table.

Lucy grinned. "He's good."

"If you don't mind me asking, what's with the name?" I interjected.

Lucy turned toward me. She was petite, almost fairy-like with her small frame, big blue eyes, and light-blond hair. She also ran a construction company with Amelia and had a bold and intimidating personality. "Levi had Ham the hamster before, but he died when he was three. We got another hamster. Levi really likes the name Ham, so..." She shrugged. In the small world of Willow Brook, Levi was also a hotshot firefighter.

I was grateful to be welcomed into this group of friends. The only downside was it seemed I might be the only single one. Tiffany had been single when I first started working at the vet clinic, but she'd fallen deeply in love with Wes. She and he were almost an insta-family as they shared guardianship of their mutual friends' son after their friends died in an accident. She had sling-shotted past being single into commitment and parenting in a matter of months.

Tiffany grinned over at Lucy. "It's cute that Levi loves hamsters." Her attention swung to me. "While we're on the subject of pets, Alice tells me that Cooper has the hots for you."

I almost choked on the swallow of water I had just taken. When I collected myself, I pointed out, "Cooper's not a pet."

She rolled her eyes. "If Alice thinks he's got the hots for you, he probably does."

"Uh, I don't think so. I expressed his cat's anal glands. Trust me, it was not my best look."

Tiffany shrugged. "It's a great way to meet someone. Before you know it, you'll have your own cat."

"I wouldn't mind having my own cat. I prefer the elderly ones, though."

"How come?" Maisie prompted as she shuffled the cards and put them away.

We had just finished our last game for the evening, which, surprisingly, Lucy won. Maisie was the most frequent winner and highly skilled at cards.

"Because the old pets are harder to find homes for. Bonus is they're usually somewhat trained, and you know what their personality is."

"That's what Wes always says," Tiffany piped up. "Should I ask him to see if the shelter has any sweet old cats?"

"Not until I'm done taking care of Humpty. We don't want to stress him out any more than he already is." I contemplated how I could carefully and casually find out more about Cooper Hughes. If anybody knew, it would be these women since most of them were married or engaged to hotshot firefighters.

Willow Brook had a surplus of hotshot firefighters since it served as a hub for several crews covering Alaska's sprawling geography, which was known for its wildfires. The side effect of all the hotshot firefighters in town was an abundance of rugged, handsome men. It was enough to overwhelm one's hormones.

The funny thing was that although I could objectively appreciate every firefighter I'd met, only Cooper lit that spark in me.

Later that evening, after Amelia graciously drove me over to Maisie's place to get Humpty and to the store for supplies, I opened Humpty's cat carrier and peered inside. He eyed me suspiciously, his round blue eyes assessing me. I stepped back. "Come out when you want. No rush," I said conversationally.

I quickly jogged back down the stairs, fetching the food, kitty litter, and the small litter box I'd picked up at the grocery store on the way home and left in the entryway. When I returned to my apartment, Humpty sat in front of his carrier. He glanced over, watching me as I poured kitty litter into the litter box and put it just inside the bathroom door beside the trash can.

I situated his food and water bowls beside the island between the kitchen and the living room. He began inspecting the area, thoroughly sniffing everything. I let my gaze arc about the space. I wouldn't have to worry about losing him in here. I lived in a small apartment on the upper floor of a building next door to Firehouse Café. Alice had hooked me up with it, and Janet James, who owned the café, was my landlord. She was the best landlord I'd ever had. There was one apartment across the hallway, but I didn't know who lived there as the last tenant had recently moved out.

It felt kind of odd to have Cooper's cat here in my apartment. I didn't know if he recognized me from our one and only meeting. He was friendly enough and kept circling back to twine around my ankles as he explored. I changed into my comfy clothes, my hand reflexively smoothing over the scar on my lower back.

My mind immediately veered to my mother, and I wondered how she was doing tonight. Lifting my phone from the coffee table, I tapped out a quick text. *Let's grab a coffee in the morning. The clinic is closed tomorrow. Say 10?*

Her reply came quickly. *I'd love that. See you then.*

———

Humpty appeared to be content the following morning. I woke with him curled up by my feet, purring up a storm. After filling his food bowl and giving him fresh water, I left, buttoning my jacket as I jogged down the stairs. The small entryway had another apartment down here that Janet told me she used for tourist rentals.

Stepping outside, I took a deep breath of the chilly air, savoring the fresh hints of spruce in the air. When my mom had told me she wanted to move to Alaska because one of her best friends lived here, I'd initially hesitated. It was a long way from California. But then, we'd both needed a change of scenery after my stepfather died.

I glanced around as I walked the short distance to Firehouse Café. Downtown Willow Brook was a cute little place. Mountains surrounded the town with snow-covered peaks stark against the blue sky. A glacier glittered under the early morning sun. The downtown area had brightly colored signs and cute storefronts. Main Street was the only street in town that had a sidewalk.

I walked into the parking area in front of Firehouse Café, smiling as I pushed through the door. The scent of fresh coffee with hints of sugar and savory flavors from the baked goods drifted through the air. It was warm in here. At this early hour, it wasn't filled with customers, but several people were at tables, reading and talking as they sipped coffee.

Local artwork was displayed on the walls in this old fire station that had been renovated into a café. The original fire pole was still here with fireweed flowers painted on it. The concrete floor was stained a soft shade of blue, and a large chalkboard hung above the register at the back with the regular menu and specials listed in colorful chalk.

I stopped at the counter, just about to reach to ring the small bell when Janet came walking through the back. She beamed when she saw me. Her dark hair streaked with silver was twisted into a braid, and her eyes crinkled at the corners with her smile.

"Good morning," I said.

"Well, good morning. Your usual?" she prompted.

"Yes, please."

Janet began to start my coffee before I added, "Give me an extra shot of espresso in that."

I usually got a triple-shot Americano, but I'd been a little restless last night with Humpty there.

"Coming right up. Didn't sleep well?" she asked.

I shrugged, wiggling my hand back and forth. "So-so. Maisie was taking care of Cooper's cat because he got called out to a fire. Apparently, their cat is not thrilled with the situation, so I took him home with me. I was a little worried, so I woke up a few times to check on him. You know how it goes."

"Well, that's convenient," she said as she tapped the button to start my coffee.

"It is?"

"Cooper's in the apartment across the hallway from you."

"Oh! I haven't seen him yet."

Janet shrugged. "Works out that way sometimes."

"It's nice you rent those apartments out to locals," I commented, well aware that many people all over the place had jumped on the short rental gravy train.

"Having regular renters who are local is a major benefit for me. I don't have time to constantly deal with people online trying to do the short-term deal," Janet explained dryly. "I'm sure Cooper will be a good neighbor." She waggled her eyebrows.

I felt the heat start to rise in my cheeks and ignored it. "He seems like a nice guy." I strived to sound bland.

Before Janet could reply, the bell on the door

jingled. I glanced over my shoulder to see my mother walking in. "Hey, Mom," I said, turning to face her as she approached.

She slipped her hand through my elbow and squeezed. "Good morning, hon."

I leaned over and kissed her on the cheek.

Janet smiled at us. "You two look so much alike."

My mother grinned as she stepped closer to the counter, releasing my arm. "We do, but I've given up on keeping my hair blond. I'm going for the natural look."

I glanced at my mother. Her once honey-blond hair had faded to white. I had gotten my coloring and build from her. We may look alike, but we were so different in other ways.

A few minutes later, we sat across from each other at a table. My mother sipped her coffee as she looked out the window. I marveled that, for the first time I could recall recently, she didn't look tense and stressed. Maybe I should've missed my stepfather, but I didn't. Not even a little. We rarely spoke of him. I didn't know if she missed him, but she was no longer under his thumb or the victim of his gaslighting and occasional physical abuse. Gerald had died in a single-car drunk-driving accident. He'd crossed the median when he was heavily intoxicated and blessedly didn't hit a single car when he barreled through the oncoming traffic. A utility pole had stopped him.

I took a swallow of my coffee, reminding myself to be grateful my mother could live peacefully now.

She met my gaze. "How are you?"

I shrugged lightly. "Fine. I'm taking care of someone's cat."

She grinned. "Maybe you should get your own cat. You always wanted one when you were growing up."

I smiled, ignoring the tightness in my chest. "I did."

What went unspoken was all of the history crammed into that one little comment. We'd had one pet, a dog my stepfather used to hit and kick. I had been the one who pushed back against Gerald. Never my mother.

My mother said nothing further about pets, but that was enough to remind me of all the ways I'd hated my childhood. Maybe, just maybe, this fresh start would kick in for me. If only I could let go of the past.

Chapter Five

COOPER

I leaned my back against my backpack propped behind me, taking a long swallow of water before lowering the bottle to the ground beside my hip. I rolled my head to the side, catching Graham's eyes.

"Long day," he offered, his tone as dry as tumbleweeds.

"Is there ever a short day when we're out in the field?" I mused with a chuckle.

"The days when we finish and wait to get picked up," Rowan chimed in.

Darkness was falling, and we had made camp for the night. Unfortunately, when fighting a wildfire, camp couldn't involve the requisite crackling campfire. Blessedly, we cleared some lines and controlled the fire today. We'd been out here for a full week. Tomorrow, we would finish up another section.

"Rain's on the way," Donovan added.

Two of the Willow Brook hotshot crews were out here with one additional hotshot crew stationed with us, all of us covering the relentlessly busy fire seasons in Alaska's sprawling landscape. Like most Western states, wildfires had become more frequent, hotter, and more challenging to control in Alaska.

"When's the rain due?" Chase asked.

"Supposed to rain tonight," Donovan replied.

Leaning my head back, I arced my gaze about the night sky. Just a glimmer of the sun was left shimmering above the outline of the mountains. Darkness enveloped the sky with a plump, almost full moon rising above. Stars glittered in the crisp air.

I'd always loved the outdoors and had grown up in the mountains of North Carolina. Alaska's mountains were something else. They towered above the landscape, unlike the mountains of the East, where you felt cradled within the valleys. Here, you could almost feel the more recent emergence of these mountains as they rose in jagged, almost intimidating peaks that boldly reached for the sky.

Nothing compared to the night sky in the wilderness. With no light pollution here, the moon was so bright it lit the landscape with a pearly glow. Even in the darkness, you could see the charred trees standing. The lingering scent of smoke hung in the air, although it was more distant now. A few hours ago, the wind had changed direction, moving the fire toward a river. Between our work of clearing lines to contain the fire and a day or two of rain, we would hopefully be able to fly home soon.

Voices rumbled quietly around me, each of us sipping from water bottles and sharing a practical dinner of protein bars, dried salmon jerky, and other portable snacks.

"Well, you've made it through three months," Rowan said from my side.

It was funny how the web of connections could bring people together in far-flung areas. A chance connection for Remy had brought Rowan here, that and the love of Rowan's life also being here. Another chance connection had brought Delilah Blake here, whose aviation mechanic husband did most of the work on the planes and helicopters that brought us in and out of the wilderness. Delilah wasn't a firefighter, but I'd already become friends with her husband as he often handled the mechanical work on the light planes and helicopters that flew us into the wilderness for work.

Although Remy wasn't on my crew, I saw him all the time. With Rowan on my crew, our friendship from Stolen Hearts Valley got stronger by the day. Remy and Rowan were solid, good men who I'd trust with my life. Those established friendships made it easier to settle into Willow Brook.

"I have," I replied, casting him a quick grin.

"Do you think you'll stay?" he prompted. Donovan was deeply in love with his wife, Jasmine. He'd told me more than once that he was here for life after moving here from out of state.

I looked back up at the stars as I replied, "Definitely. I needed the change of scenery, but it's pretty easy to fall in love with Alaska."

When my gaze met Donovan's again, he nodded in agreement. "It was an easy call for me to stay here."

"You're also whipped," Graham Holden, our crew's superintendent, offered with a chuckle.

"Same goes for you," Donovan countered with a grin.

I glanced around, mentally noting that many guys here were happily shacked up. Maybe I was falling in love with Alaska, but I didn't intend to fall in love with a human. Not ever again.

"Won't take Cooper long," Rowan offered. "Someone's due as it is."

"Won't take me long to do what?" I prompted.

"It's a thing," Rowan said. "Everyone who comes here stays here because they fall in love. I think it's in the water."

"Most people in Alaska have well water," Chase added with a roll of his eyes.

I looked among the group, shaking my head. "I might fall in love with Alaska, but I'm *not* falling in love. I have no intention of ever getting married."

"What do you have against love?" Beck Steele asked as he approached, dropping his gear bag down and sitting in front of it, using it as a rest for his elbows as he leaned back.

I'd only been around the station in Willow Brook for about a week before I realized that Beck was the hotshot firefighter equivalent of the office gossip. That said, he was a nice guy and solid and reliable in the field. He was married to Maisie from the station.

"I don't have anything against love. I've already been in love. Been there, done that. My fiancée fucked one of my friends after my father died. Said I wasn't emotionally available. I don't need to go through that bullshit again."

Beck looked sincerely pained on my behalf. "I'm sorry. That fucking sucks. Whoever the guy was, he wasn't your friend."

"Clearly not." I ignored the bitter sting of pain in my heart.

"I get where you're coming from, but you just never know what might happen. I never thought I'd fall in love, and look at me now," Beck offered with a shrug.

My brows hitched up as I studied him. "Dude,

you're a total family man. I've seen you with Maisie and your kids."

"He wasn't always," Graham piped up. "Beck was a total flirt in high school."

"Probably the worst flirt in school," Chase added.

"I can promise you this," Beck began. "Not one of these guys here would ever fuck someone you were with."

"Good to know, but there's no chance of that even being something for me to worry about."

The conversation moved on, and I was relieved. I didn't like to dwell on what had happened. There was cheating, and then there was nuclear cheating. What happened was a next-level betrayal. Even worse, it was all tangled up in my grief over my father dying. I mentally scoffed when I remembered my ex's words.

"You've been depressed. You've hardly been available for me," Cindy had said.

She'd said that with a straight face a mere two months after my father died unexpectedly. What the fuck?

My mind spun to Farrah. I still couldn't believe my reaction to her. Maybe I wouldn't fall in love, but I sure as hell wouldn't mind a distraction.

Chapter Six

COOPER

A few days later, we filtered into the station after three helicopters delivered us home to Willow Brook. We were all tired and filthy, and it was good to be home. We'd left with the fire fully contained. Even though the work was hard, dangerous, and grueling at times, I loved it. There was a satisfaction to it.

After a long, hot shower, I dressed and walked out to the front of the station. Beck stood at the counter, and Maisie laughed at something he had said. For just a moment, I felt like I had walked in on a private moment. A counter separated them, and they weren't even doing anything to question. At a glance, they could've been two strangers. But I could feel the intimacy shimmering between them and the look of familiarity and love they shared.

Once upon a time, not even all that long ago, I'd believed I'd had something like that. I thought I'd wanted it. A familiar sting scored across my heart. The wounds of that double betrayal still hadn't scarred over completely. I didn't miss my ex, but the betrayal stung.

Beck glanced over his shoulder, his smile encompassing me. "Hey there. Want to go out to Wildlands with us?"

"I need to get my cat. Maisie took care of him for me."

"Oh, that's right," Beck replied.

"How's Humpty doing?" I looked over at her.

"Oh!" she exclaimed. "Farrah has him, the vet tech. She said you knew her. Our cat was really cranky about Humpty. When we had card night, she offered to take him. Trust me, it was best for Humpty," Maisie said earnestly.

"Oh, no problem. I'm just glad he's safe with someone."

Maisie let out a sigh of relief. "I was worried you would think I didn't want to care for him."

"Maisie," I said as I stopped beside Beck at the counter that encircled her desk, "You took Humpty on really short notice. I'm just grateful."

Just then, Wes, the guy whose mom ran the rescue program where I had gotten Humpty, appeared from the back hallway, hearing the tail end of our conversation. "How is Humpty?" he asked.

"I guess I'll find out. Farrah, the vet tech, took him."

"Ah, well, he's in good hands. I know Farrah. They do all the vet care for the rescue program," he explained.

"Do you happen to know how to get ahold of her? Should I just call the clinic?" I asked. My eyes bounced to the clock mounted above the door into the back hallway. "I'm guessing they're closed."

"I have Farrah's number." Maisie whipped her phone out. "I'm texting it to you right now. Just tell her I gave it to you. I'm sure it won't be too weird. Be nice," she ordered.

I held my palms up. "Of course, I'll be nice. I promise. I'll even be grateful."

My phone vibrated with Maisie's text. Maisie had shared her contact with me. Farrah was labeled *Gorgeous Farrah*.

I was just about to open my mouth and agree with her when I thought better of it. Beck happened to glance down at my screen and snorted. "Maisie has nicknames for everyone."

"What's my name?" I couldn't help but ask.

"Coopy Coop," Maisie said with a grin.

I chuckled. "Okay. I wasn't asking to be gorgeous, but..."

Maisie rolled her eyes. "This fire station is full of hotshot firefighters. Most of you are handsome. Beck is the only one who gets to me. Plus, most of my friends are crushing on or married to the others, so I can't be using inappropriate names for the guys. I think everyone would agree that Farrah fits the gorgeous description." She punctuated that with a firm nod.

Just then, Susannah, one of the female firefighters, came walking out of the back hallway and caught her last comment. "I completely concur. Farrah is totally gorgeous. None of the guys will say anything about it because they know better."

Wes snorted. "I'd like to know my nickname."

Maisie scrolled through her phone contacts, looking up. "Wessie Wes."

"Is there a theme here?" I prompted. "Is Beck Becky Beck?"

Maisie burst out laughing. "Nope, he is Beck Action Hero Steele."

Beck rolled his eyes, looking a little sheepish. "Because my name is Beck Steele, she says I sound like an action hero."

"You do, but I got that from Carrie Dodge." She winked. "Carrie said your name sounds like an action hero's name. It totally does."

"Wow, I even know who Carrie is," I teased.

"It's a training requirement to go with the town crew to rescue Carrie's cat." Beck grinned.

I cuffed Beck lightly on the shoulder. "Dude, I think the name fits. Plus, you're a hotshot firefighter, so technically, you're also an action hero."

Amid a chorus of laughter, I departed. Maisie's text with Farrah's number burned a hole in my pocket where my phone was nestled as I walked out to my truck. I decided to stop by my apartment before I texted her.

It was a short drive down Main Street, and I pulled into the parking area behind Firehouse Café, which shared a parking lot with where I lived. My footsteps echoed as I jogged up the stairs. Cresting the landing, I turned down the hallway. I happened to be looking down when I heard my name.

I whipped my head up to see Farrah Taylor standing in the hallway with her keys. "Cooper?" she prompted again.

I came to an abrupt stop a few feet away from her in the hallway. "Hi. I was planning to text you. Maisie gave me your contact information. What are you doing here?"

She pointed toward the doorway across the hallway from my apartment. "I live here. I only found out you'd moved in while you were gone."

My gaze traveled down the hallway before it returned to her. "I guess you're my neighbor then."

She nodded slowly. My eyes, greedy and hungry for a thorough look at her, took in the way her honey-blond hair was pulled up in a ponytail. Several locks had fallen loose along her neck. The glasses she had on today served to set off her green eyes. She wore a pair of overalls over a fitted T-shirt. Even though everything she wore was loose except the T-shirt, all it did was rev the engine of my curiosity. I felt like every cell in my body fired, sending heat sizzling through me.

"When did you move in?" Farrah prompted.

"A few weeks ago. I haven't seen you or whoever's downstairs yet. Actually, is there anyone downstairs?"

"Janet says that's the fancy place. She rents it out to tourists, so it's a rotating cast of characters. Up here, it's just us. The last person moved out last month, and I wondered when Janet would rent it out again."

"It's good to have a neighbor I know. Maisie told me what happened. Thanks for taking care of Humpty."

"I can do it anytime. I'm just across the hall. Honestly, if you prefer for me just to feed him when you're out of town—"

I cut in. "He likes attention. I haven't had him that long and hadn't sorted out plans for him when I'm out for a fire."

"I get it. Come on in. You can see him." She unlocked her door, pausing with her hand on the doorknob.

"I was going to pop into my apartment and make sure I had enough litter and food. I moved in a rush, and honestly, I can't remember."

She waved a hand dismissively as she opened her door. "I have plenty."

With that, I followed her in. I glanced around,

mentally noting her place was a mirror of mine. The main area was an open living space with the living room to the front and facing the street with a small island serving as a divider between that and the kitchen at the back. I presumed the two doors to the side were the bathroom and bedroom, just like my place.

As I glanced around, my gaze landed on Humpty on the back of the sofa, looking out the window at the street. He looked over and quickly leaped off the couch, trotting across the room and circling my ankles and then Farrah's.

I leaned down to greet him. "Hey, dude," I said conversationally, scratching under his chin.

He replied with a rumbling purr. Farrah smiled at us when I glanced up at her. "He is generous with his purring," she offered.

"Any problems with him?" I straightened.

She leaned down and scooped him up in her arms, stroking over the top of his head. "Not a one. He definitely likes his attention. I've just been feeding him and changing the litter box. Cats are pretty easy to take care of. Dogs are too, but they actually involve walking. I also got Humpty some catnip toys." She waggled her eyebrows. "He loves them."

I chuckled. "Good to know. I got a scratching post for him, but he hasn't shown much interest. I'll have to try the catnip toys."

"Hang on. I have a basket for him." She lowered Humpty to the floor and turned to set her purse and keys on the island counter. "Here are his toys." Farrah walked over and lifted a small basket off the floor. Returning to me, she handed it over. I looked inside to see a collection of stuffed animals, all with bells attached. "They're all stuffed with catnip. He loves them. And there's this." She lifted what appeared to be a small fishing rod that had a line with a toy attached to the end. She held it up, swinging it back and forth. Humpty came dashing over to leap in the air and bat happily at it. "It'll keep him entertained. I even got you one of those little penlight things for him." She demonstrated that as well with Humpty running around and chasing the dot of light on the floor.

I smiled sheepishly. "I think you're a better cat parent than I am."

Farrah placed the pen back in the basket and shrugged. "Not really. I just like wasting money on cat toys."

"All done fighting that fire?" she asked, resting her hips against the counter as she turned to face me again.

I took a few steps, stopping beside her. "All done."

I could literally feel the voltage in the space between us, like a charge about to go off.

She blinked and pushed her glasses up on her nose. "Aside from helping with Humpty, if you need anything..." She paused and shrugged. Just then, her stomach growled. Farrah's cheeks went pink, and she pressed her palm over her stomach. "I'm starving. I was just about to order takeout. Do you want some?"

No fucking way would I turn that down. All I wanted was to spend more time with Farrah.

"I was thinking of ordering from the Gallery Café. It's curry night there," she added.

"Sounds good to me. Do they deliver?"

At her nod, I replied, "Let's order then. I'm not up for going anywhere. I'll pop across the hall and drop off my bag. I'd say we could eat over there, but I'm not too organized. I'm so glad the place came furnished."

Farrah grinned. "I know. It's a handy feature."

I looked around, taking in the colorful throw pillows on the couch and the artwork on the walls. Her apartment had more personal touches even though the furnishings were the same as mine. I glanced at her, casting a sheepish grin. "I think you're better at decorating than me."

"I'm sure you did just fine."

After conferring on the order and telling Farrah I'd eat whatever she recommended, I stepped across the hall. When I turned on the lights, I glanced around. I dropped my bag in the bathroom by the washer and dryer, planning to start a load of laundry before I went to bed.

I checked the kitchen cabinet I had designated for Humpty's food to discover I still had half a bag of cat food left and plenty of litter in the bathroom for him. When I returned to Farrah's apartment, she offered me a beer.

A few minutes later, we were seated, and I discovered that the loveseat was small. Even though she tucked herself in the corner, it felt like she was immediately beside me. Humpty sat behind us on the top of the cushions, purring up a storm.

The food was as delicious as Farrah promised. I didn't want to leave after we finished eating. I had expected this to be an evening of tension and perhaps awkward conversation. Instead, Farrah was remarkably easy to talk with. She had a litany of questions about firefighting.

Throughout the evening, the underlying thrumming hum of attraction never abated. Finally, my rational brain kicked in and told me to get the hell out of there. I managed to stand and tell her I should go.

She stood with me, looking up. My eyes were

drawn to her mouth like a bee to honey. Before I knew it, I was taking another step, lifting a hand and brushing my knuckles along her cheek. All the while, my heartbeat pounded along.

Chapter Seven

FARRAH

Cooper stared down at me, and I felt lost in his dark gaze. Everything about tonight had been unexpected. Here we were, a few hours later, and I didn't want him to leave. Being with him was easy. I'd expected it to feel strained and bumbling. I'd never been great at dating.

Not that this is a date, the well-trained, cynical side of my mind pointed out.

I'd never even had a serious relationship. Life had taught me one thing—sure as sugar, you couldn't trust a man.

I'd also learned thoroughly from my mother's marriage to my stepfather. My father had passed away when I was too young to remember him. After my mother remarried Gerald, a wealthy attorney from a family with plenty of money, I learned that what someone showed you wasn't usually the whole story. What Gerald seemed like and what he was were two different pictures.

I didn't trust myself to be vulnerable with anyone. Vulnerability left you at risk of being manipulated, falling for the good side of someone when the bad side dictated their life and yours when all was said and done.

Against all odds, I felt safe with Cooper. There was an ease, a lightness to how I felt with him. He exuded an almost protective quality that I just wanted to sink into.

At this very moment, he was less than a foot away from me, and the brush of his knuckles on my cheek felt like the lick of a flame over the surface of my skin. The heat radiated outward and spun into the fire, simmering on a low burn inside me. Butterflies massed in my belly, sending tingles scattering through me. My pulse raced, and my breath was shallow. Oh. My. God. I wanted this man to kiss me like I'd never wanted anything in my life.

I could hear the echoing drumroll of my heartbeat and the rush of blood in my ears. I could feel the heat and liquid need sliding through my veins and sparks dancing over the surface of my skin. Cooper's dark eyes skated over my face, and I tried to take a breath.

His knuckles trailed down my cheek and along my jawline. I felt as if I stood on the edge of a precipice, just about to topple over. It was a sense of rushing, of anticipation, a gathering force of energy. I made a little sound at the back of my throat.

I didn't know who made the next move, but we leaned toward each other. Cooper's heat encompassed the space around us. Unable to stop myself, I lifted my hand, trailing my fingertips along the stubbled edge of his jaw before I leaned forward and pressed a kiss just below his jaw.

When my lips landed against his skin, my entire system felt jolted by a hot shock. I abruptly realized what I'd done, but Cooper's hand slid into my hair before I could even think beyond that. His eyes met mine, the look there blazing hot just before he brought his lips to mine.

Maybe it was him, perhaps it was me, or maybe it was the rushing need inside me, but the simple act of kissing Cooper made me weak-kneed, nearly melting me like ice under the hot sun. The kiss started out gentle. His lips brushed over mine once and then again. He dropped a kiss at one corner of my mouth and then the other. All the while, I felt absolutely wild inside, an intensity of sensation kicking up like a storm.

He spoke against my lips. "I want you, Farrah."

"I want you too," I whispered in return.

In another moment, he angled his head to the side, his mouth slanting over mine as he claimed it. His tongue swept in boldly, stealing my very breath. Another moment later, he lifted his head, and we stood there, staring at each other.

I could feel the rapid beat of his heart against my palm where it had landed over his chest. My heartbeat raced wildly out of control as well. We both breathed rapidly, the sound filling the air around us.

Humpty's meowing snapped through the moment. Cooper held my gaze for another few beats before taking a step back. "I should go," he finally said.

It was all I could do not to fist my hand in his shirt and hold him right there in front of me. Wordlessly, I nodded.

I didn't want him to go. Not at all.

Chapter Eight

FARRAH

That kiss replayed on a loop in my mind a while later until I managed to fall into a restless sleep. I told myself it was just a fluke. A crazy moment that would never *ever* happen again. It couldn't. It shouldn't. Therefore, I wouldn't let it happen.

I resolved to forget it. My attempts to kick Cooper out of my thoughts were running up against the reality of him living across the hallway from me. I didn't even see him for the next two days, but it took an effort not to leap up and run to the door when I heard his footsteps in the hallway. I didn't usually hang around at home, wondering what my neighbors were doing. That just wasn't my thing. Now, it was totally my thing. What the hell was wrong with me?

I pondered how different his apartment looked from mine. I wondered how Humpty was doing, and I kind of missed the little guy. He was an older cat and sort of scrunchy looking, but he was sweet and funny.

I also told myself I didn't need to mention that kiss to anyone. Kisses meant nothing in my book. At the ancient age of ten, I had sworn off men.

As if to remind me of all the reasons, I was having coffee with my mother again, something we had fallen into the habit of doing once a week. I loved my mother. She was all I had left when it came to family. Somewhere out there, I supposed I had some family connected to him, but I didn't know much about my father's family, and he was an only child. My mother's parents had long ago lost contact with her. I assumed it was because of my stepfather. When I'd dared to ask, my mother had looked so devastated that I couldn't press for more.

My mother and I tried to be close, and we were in some ways. But maintaining our relationship meant certain topics were off-limits. It was as if a force field that neither one of us dared to cross surrounded those topics. On occasion, we stumbled through those force fields by accident.

When my mother sat down across from me, I wasn't thinking when I asked, "Are you okay?"

Her eyes were red as if she'd been crying. She traced her thumb in a circle around her coffee cup. "Your stepfather died two years ago today. I miss him."

My heartbeat picked up its pace, and not in a good way. It was this unsteady, familiar, and frightened beat. I wanted to take my mother by the shoulders and shake her. For the first time since I could remember, my mother had a full two years of her life when she didn't bear a bruise left by my stepfather. I tried to understand what had happened. I truly did.

Intellectually, I knew why she missed Gerald. I understood that love was complicated and messy and that she had loved the parts of him that weren't abusive. I also understood that holding that love was a way to help people tolerate an experience of abuse. It hadn't been safe for her to leave him when he was alive. I knew the statistics. It was perilous for women to try to escape abusive relationships. In fact, during and after an attempt to leave was the most dangerous time in abusive relationships, and more women died.

I could recite all of those facts in my brain, and I could remind myself that I loved the part of my mother that didn't cling to a memory of my stepfather that didn't exist. But it still hurt. There was a good reason we tiptoed around this topic.

Before I could think better of it, I asked, "Do you remember my birthday when I was ten?"

My mother stared at me, her nostrils flaring as she took an unsteady breath. I saw the pain in her eyes, laced with guilt and regret. Or so I thought.

"Of course, I do," she said hoarsely. "Like I've told you before, I know everything Gerald did wrong. I know it doesn't make sense that I miss him. But I do."

Even though it felt like pounding my fist against a door, locked and bolted shut, the part of me that still wanted to fight the situation persisted just a little bit more. "Mom, I had to call the police that time he pushed you down the stairs. He threw my birthday cupcake at the wall."

Whenever I spoke that detail aloud, it felt small. Yet, it wasn't. It was just one of hundreds of times when my step-dad blew up over minor things. It was the weight of fear, the endless tiptoeing around to keep him from spiraling out of control. Simply talking about it exhausted me. That's what the world didn't understand about abuse. The big, bad events were never the only things happening. It was the constant drip, drip, drip of control and fear that wore you down and left you emotionally spent.

"You always ask me why I don't date. Well, I made a promise to myself that day. I would never, *never*—" My voice came out low and forceful as I blinked back tears. "—have to worry about anything like that ever again."

My mother took a quick breath, letting it out in a sigh. She swallowed audibly before squaring her shoulders. "I'm sorry."

And I knew she was. I knew she felt bad about all of it. Her guilt had clung to her when he was alive, and we still lived with him. I immediately felt horrible for saying anything. I supposed it was better for her to remember only the good parts of my stepfather. It was just that I couldn't remember any good parts. The stretches of time with no violence were almost worse because I was always waiting—waiting for him to blow up, waiting for how bad it might be, and wishing he would just go away.

I reached across the table, curling my hand over hers, squeezing it quickly, and releasing it before leaning back in my chair. "I know you are, Mom. I'm sorry. I shouldn't have said anything. I know we can't change what happened." That knowledge was concrete and true. Yet a corner of my heart still wished I could change the past. I wished I could will away everything that had gone so very wrong.

She studied me quietly for a moment. "You can say something. I just hope you understand. There are many things about Gerald that I don't miss, but I still miss him. No one person is all good or bad."

I blinked, willing myself not to cry as I felt tears stinging the backs of my eyes.

She held my gaze steadily. Sometimes it annoyed me that she had found some peace. I didn't know if I ever would.

Just when I thought this brief conversation couldn't get any worse, I happened to glance to my side and discover that Cooper sitting there with Jonah and Wes, both friends of mine, because they were in love with the closest friends I had in town.

I didn't even know when they sat down there, but I could tell by the look on Cooper's face he had heard what I'd said about Gerald. One of the best things about coming to Willow Brook was that I felt like I'd found a fresh start. I'd finally closed the door on that ugly part of my life, a part I had no control over. As my mother pointed out, you couldn't change the past. I knew that as permanently as if it were burned into my skin.

When my mother suggested moving to Alaska to stay with her friend, I jumped at the chance to get us out of that house filled with ghosts and memories. That house I hadn't been able to leave because I'd wanted to protect my mother. After Gerald died, I wanted to make sure she was okay, so I stayed.

My small apartment here was my very first place alone. I had just turned thirty. I didn't want people here to know the ugly history of my stepfather. And now, I feared Cooper did.

I smiled tightly and looked away. My mother knew me well. She was also an absolute expert at deftly changing the subject and pretending everything was fine. She had built her entire life around that. Without missing a beat, she shifted gears. "I'm buying that house."

"You are?" I prompted, injecting brightness into my tone. I could fake it as well as she could.

"Yes, Shelly and I are going halfsies on the deposit."

"Are you sure—" I began before my mother cut in.

"I'm positive. I made plenty of money when I sold our house in San Francisco. I've known Shelly forever. I can never thank her enough for what she did for me here. I like having a roommate. I don't really want to live alone. I think I'm too old for that at this point."

I took a swallow of my coffee, savoring the bitterness and the jolt of caffeine. "Well then, I think it's great. Let me know what I can do to help."

"It's a three bedroom, so if you wanted to stay..." My mother's words trailed off when I shook my head.

"Mom, I have my own place for the first time, and I love it."

She smiled. "That's what I told Shelly you would say."

Our conversation moved along. When I finally risked a glance at Cooper, he was laughing at something Jonah had said. My mother got up to go to the restroom, and I told her I had to go to work. That was the truth, insofar as I did need to go to work even if I would be arriving early. Mostly, I just wanted to escape the threat of an awkward interaction with Cooper.

I stood from the table, slipping into my jacket and looping my purse strap over my shoulder. "Hey, Farrah," Wes said as I turned. "I heard you took good care of Humpty. Do you want a cat?"

I laughed. "I swear, Wes, if rescue animals were drugs, I would say you were a dealer."

Cooper and Jonah laughed at that comment while Wes grinned and shrugged. "I get it. My mom always sends me updates on the new arrivals there. You're a vet tech, so I know they'll get the best care."

"I'll think about it." I managed to greet Jonah and Cooper casually like it was no big deal that they might've just heard me reveal an ugly truth about my life.

As I walked away, my eyes stung with tears, and a sense of weary anger rolled through me in a slow wave. I was so tired of wishing for a different past.

Chapter Nine

COOPER

My gaze tracked Farrah as she walked out of the café. A swirl of cool air blew inside as the door swung shut behind her. When I looked away, I collided with Wes's gaze. If he thought anything of me watching her, he didn't comment on it. I took a swallow of my coffee, feeling unsettled by what I'd overheard Farrah say to the woman I presumed to be her mother.

I sensed Wes and Jonah had heard just as much as I had. The tables in here were close together. When Farrah's voice had risen, I hadn't wanted to listen, but it had been impossible to tune out. I hated knowing that detail about her childhood.

While I wondered what to say to my friends, a voice came from behind my shoulder. "Well, hey guys," Remy drawled.

I was relieved for the interruption and glanced up at him when he stopped beside our table. "Hey, man," I replied. "Here for coffee?"

Remy cracked a grin. "Of course."

Just then, his wife caught up to him. Rachel was pretty with brown hair, blue eyes, and an outdoorsy, warm vibe. She smiled among us. "Good morning, guys." Her gaze lingered on me. "Well, it's been, what? Three months now? How do you like Willow Brook?"

I cocked my head to the side. "I like it. Rumor has it I'm gonna have to make it through a few winters before anyone will believe I'm tough enough to stay."

Jonah snorted beside me. "It's true."

"Are you from here?" I prompted. I was still learning the details of my crew members' lives here.

Jonah shook his head. "Not really. My dad grew up here, but he moved away. He and my mom moved back just recently. We used to spend summers up here. The people who grew up here don't think that counts," he said with an easy shrug.

Wes chuckled. "I grew up here and moved away. There *are* difficult winters in other places."

Remy nodded. "The Upper Midwest is freaking brutal in the winter. I think it's colder there than it is here. Technically, we're in the southern part of Alaska. The winters here are a little colder than average, but it's not so bad. Winter is definitely darker and longer, though." He glanced at me, adding, "The winters in the mountains of North Carolina aren't as cold, but you'll be able to deal with the weather just fine here. Especially if you like the snow."

"You know I love snow." Remy and I used to ski together in the winters in North Carolina. It wasn't always great snow for skiing because it tended to be wet rather than dry powder, but we loved it anyway. "I'm looking forward to better snow here."

"Oh, you'll get plenty of powder here," Wes chimed in. "There's a ski resort in Diamond Creek, a few hours south of here."

"I heard about that. Delilah told me that's how she met Alex," I commented.

Rachel smiled. "We gave her some comp tickets we had. She flew out here and skidded off the highway on her drive to Diamond Creek. Alex stopped to help her. He was her high school crush from summer camp."

"Small fucking world," Remy said with a grin.

Rachel nudged him with her elbow. "I'm gonna go get in line."

"Right there with you. See you guys later," he said as he turned and walked away.

Although Remy had hooked me up with a job here, he was on a different hotshot crew, but I still saw him plenty. We all crossed paths in the small town when we weren't in the field together.

We filtered out of the café not much later, and I returned to the station to work out. I was in the kitchen area in the back of the station when I saw Maisie walking by with her arms filled with paper boxes. "Need some help?" I called over.

She glanced my way with a sheepish smile. "Actually, I do. I overestimated how much I could carry and didn't realize I would need at least one free hand to open the door."

I set my water bottle down and crossed over, quickly divesting her of everything she was carrying.

"You don't have to get everything," she protested.

"One of us needs to open the door," I returned with a shrug.

A moment later, I set the boxes of paper down behind Maisie's desk, where she directed me to put them. I straightened and walked back around to the front of her desk.

"How's Humpty, by the way?" She sat at her desk, tapping a key on her keyboard and looking up at me expectantly.

"He's doing great. By the way, thank you again for

making sure he had someone to take care of him while I was gone."

"Now, you have Farrah whenever you need her. You're right across the hallway from her, right?"

I nodded, wondering where she'd heard that.

As if she could read my thoughts, Maisie added, "Farrah mentioned you moved in across from her. Those are cute apartments."

Clearly, Maisie and Farrah were friendly. I had so many questions about Farrah, and this level of curiosity was unsettling for me. I wanted to know if Maisie knew Farrah's stepfather had thrown a cupcake against the wall on her birthday. I wanted to know if she knew all the details about Farrah I didn't know.

Fuck. This was exactly the kind of thing I didn't need to be wondering about any woman.

"She's single," Maisie said, seemingly out of nowhere.

"Huh?"

Maisie gave off an innocent vibe. With her curly brown hair, her big brown eyes, and her freckled cheeks, she seemed friendly and kind. And she was. But she also knew freaking everything about everyone in town, as far as I could tell.

She grinned, waggling her eyebrows. "Farrah's totally gorgeous. Plus, you're not seeing anyone."

"And how would you know that?" I countered.

She shrugged, all innocent-like. "I know lots of things."

"Relationships aren't my thing," I said, wishing I could ignore the way my heart twisted at that. I'd never been that kind of guy before. I had wanted to settle down and start a family. Until I learned betrayal came when you least expected it.

Maisie held my gaze for a moment, her eyes

widening slightly in surprise. "Oh," she said. She opened her mouth to say something further when a call came in. She whipped her headset on to answer the call. I walked into the back again, my mind replaying Farrah's comment to her mother.

I dwelled on that detail, wondering what else had happened to her. I'd hated the look in Farrah's eyes when she'd glanced over and noticed us beside her.

Chapter Ten

COOPER

I kept hoping I'd see Farrah in the hallway, but several days passed before I finally did. I crested the top of the stairs to hear her say, "Oh, shit!"

Her exclamation was followed by something falling to the floor in a clatter. Turning into the hallway, I found her kneeling with groceries spilled around her.

"Need some help?" I asked as I approached in quick strides, stopping beside her and bending down to gather up two cans that had rolled away.

She looked up at me and let out a huff. "I suppose I do." Her lips kicked up at one corner. "Thank you."

A few minutes later, we had the groceries back in the bags. I held the door open for her as she walked into her apartment.

"I overestimated how much I could carry," she said over her shoulder as I followed her inside, carrying two bags.

"It happens," I replied lightly. I set the bags where she directed on the kitchen island.

I studied her as she put a few items in the refrigerator. Yet again, I recalled what she'd said to her mother. That detail had elicited a fierce sense of protectiveness inside. I knew her stepfather was gone because I'd heard that too. I knew he couldn't hurt her again. Maybe I personally hadn't experienced anything like that, but I knew what it was like to have someone hurt you. I also knew the scars would always be there, even if something was over.

Farrah turned to look at me, smoothing a hand over her mussed hair. This was the first time I'd seen her with her hair down. It fell in tousled waves around her shoulders. It was thick and luxurious. I wanted to step closer, slide my hands into it, and kiss her.

She blinked up at me when she stopped in front of me. "How are you?"

Her question was perfectly normal, but it felt like everything with Farrah was weighted with a charge. My body was primed, and need was cracking its whip through the air and snapping into the electricity shimmering around us.

I cleared my throat. "Fine. You?"

She cocked her head to the side, a slow smile unfurling and drawing my eyes down to her mouth. Fuck me. Her lips were so perfectly kissable. Her bottom lip was a little plumper than the top one. I only now noticed that she had a tiny, barely-there dimple that peeked out on one side when she smiled.

I dragged my eyes back up to hers as she replied, "Fine. Are we in the 'fine' stage of friendship?" she asked lightly.

"What's the 'fine' stage of friendship?" I quipped.

The motion of her fingertip tracing along the edge of the counter caught my eye. I sensed she was a little nervous.

She took a quick breath, shrugging. "I'm not sure."

"I'm not either, but you took care of my cat, and I

can't stop thinking about kissing you." What slipped out next startled me. "And I'd like to throat-punch your stepfather."

Farrah's eyes widened, a flash of pain entering her gaze before it disappeared quickly. She looked down and then back up. "I thought maybe you guys heard that." Her soft voice was threaded with discomfort.

"I didn't mean to hear it."

Her mouth twisted to the side. "It's okay. It's kind of hard not to overhear people there, and I think I might've been a little loud."

"I'm sorry. Really."

I wanted to fold her into my arms and hold her close and slay every dragon she'd ever faced. All for her.

Her eyes searched mine for a moment, and I wasn't sure how to interpret the look held there. "I'm sorry too. We can't change the past. Maybe you didn't hear all of it, but he's dead. I feel like an asshole because I don't miss him, and I'm mad that my mother even does."

"No one deserves a stepfather like that."

She nodded in agreement. After a moment of quiet began to stretch, she added, "Well then, that was freaking awkward."

When she rolled her eyes, I nodded, still caught in a riptide of protectiveness for her. "Yeah."

"Maybe we should talk about our kiss," she teased. "That's awkward too, but it's not awful." Her lips curled with a sly smile, and I sensed she *really* didn't want to dwell on her stepfather.

She bit her bottom lip as she looked up at me. And, holy hell, the sight of her teeth catching the corner and denting the plush, pink surface sent a fiery sizzle down my spine.

"Is that all? It just wasn't awful? Because if that's the case, I need to try again," I teased.

We stared at each other. It felt as if a storm was rushing into the air with lightning sizzling, thunder rolling, and a burgeoning sense of pressure building between us.

"Oh, it was far from awful." Her husky response sent heat blazing through me.

She took a step toward me, and I met her halfway. "Oh, well, good to know," I murmured.

Her cheeks were tinged pink. All we were doing was standing there, inches away from each other, and it felt like foreplay. I could feel the swell of my cock and the way my balls tightened. My heart kicked harder and faster inside my chest.

"I think we should try again. Just to check," she whispered.

Her tongue darted out, sliding across her bottom lip. I took another half step. Our bodies were touching now. It felt as if a force field surrounded us. Her jacket was unzipped, and she wore a thin blouse underneath. I could feel the tight peaks of her nipples against my chest. Her lips parted as she looked up at me, and I could barely think above my roar of desire.

Chapter Eleven

COOPER

For one blazing second, we froze, simply staring at each other. Farrah's palm fell to my chest. I knew she could feel the rapid beat of my heart. I lifted a hand, sliding my fingers through her silky soft hair and letting my palm slip down to rest on the side of her neck.

I could feel the wild thrum of her pulse just along the base of my thumb. She swallowed, the sound audible in the quiet space of her kitchen. Then she bit her bottom lip again, her teeth catching on the plush surface. Her lashes swept down, and I heard the sound of her breath hitch in the back of her throat. That barely-there sound sent another fiery sizzle of electricity straight to my balls. I ached with need for her.

When her teeth released her bottom lip, I dipped my head and brushed my lips over hers, the soft, glancing touch hardly anything. Yet *everything* with Farrah — every touch, every look, every second in her presence — was imbued with an intense sense of connection twined within fierce desire.

I felt the rise of her breath as her soft curves

pressed against me. "Cooper," she gasped. The hint of a plea laced my name.

"Yes?"

"Kiss me, please." This time, her voice was still a whisper, but that whisper was a clear order.

It was a given that I was going to kiss her. The only thing up in the air was just how far it would go from the starting point.

"As you wish," I murmured against her lips before claiming her mouth.

Untrammeled need pounded through me. Farrah let out a little sigh into our kiss as her mouth opened underneath mine. I stepped closer, sliding my hand down the side of her neck, over her shoulder, and in a sweeping pass along her spine. My palm came to rest at the sweet dip of her waist. My fingers splayed over the curve of her bottom as I pulled her closer.

I let out a growl just as she let out a whimper. Our tongues tangled, and our kiss went wild. She smelled sweet, almost like sugar with a hint of vanilla. She sighed again, and I couldn't get enough. I breathed her in, taking deep sips of her, savoring the way she kissed me boldly as if she'd thrown her restraint away in the wind.

I lost all sense of time, having no idea how long our kiss lasted. We broke apart abruptly, both of us sucking in deep gulps of air. We stared at each other. Her lips were parted as she breathed rapidly.

We were plastered together, and I didn't want even a centimeter to separate us. Yet I needed more; I wanted more; I wanted more of Farrah than I wanted air. I couldn't even think. Everything that drove me was instinct and raw need. I stepped back just enough to glance down.

Another moment later, I shoved her jacket off her

shoulders. It fell to the floor in a rumple behind her as I rasped, "I need to see you."

I tugged roughly at the buttons on her blouse, swearing and then shifting gears as I turned. I slid my hands down over the sweet curves of her hips and lifted her onto the counter. Her knees splayed open, and I stepped between them. For a moment, I rested my palms flat on the counter and looked into her dark-green gaze.

"You can tell me to stop at any point."

She blinked, the tinge of pink on her cheeks deepening. She shook her head. "I don't want you to stop. I don't want us to stop. Not yet."

She lifted her hands to her blouse, deftly unbuttoning it. My cock swelled to the point of pain when her blouse fell open. I discovered she was wearing this lacy concoction of a bra, leaving her pink nipples visible through the creamy white lace. She reached between us, her palm stroking over the hard length of my cock through my jeans, sending a shot of blood arrowing there.

I gritted my teeth. "Fuck," I groaned, need lashing through me.

Dipping my head, I sucked one of her nipples into my mouth, savoring the way she cried out sharply. Her fingers speared into my hair as I sucked lightly, dampening the lace over her nipple.

A second later, we were kissing again as I pulled her to the edge of the counter until my cock nestled in the cradle of her hips. I could feel the heat of her arousal there.

I couldn't get enough of Farrah—of the sweet taste of her mouth, of her scent, of the way she kissed with abandon, of her tongue tangling with mine. Nothing felt orchestrated. Everything felt like a wild rush, the breaking of a dam in spring.

She wore these soft, stretchy leggings. My hand slid from the plump weight of her breast over the soft curve of her belly, behind her waistband, and between her thighs, finding the silk of her panties wet. Pushing them to the side, I delved into her slippery core, feeling a surge of gratification at the way she let out a needy whimper when she broke free from my mouth. Her lips parted, and I watched her as I sank one finger and then another inside her rippling, clenching channel.

Her breath came in shallow pants as she rocked into my touch. Her eyes fell closed, lifting slowly when I said, "I need to see you."

It was maybe not even a minute when I felt her begin to tighten around my fingers. I finally teased my thumb over the swollen bud of her clit. She cried out sharply, and I held her against me. She shuddered and trembled around me.

I was startled at how giving her this pleasure was *everything* I wanted at this moment. Oh, I wouldn't deny I might've sold my very soul to bury myself in her slick heat, to fuse myself with her. But this, *her* pleasure, was all I wanted just now. I wanted to savor it. I wanted to wait for more because then it would be all that much *more*.

Chapter Twelve

FARRAH

My head was tucked into the curve of Cooper's neck, and I breathed him in. He smelled earthy and musky with a hint of crisp, cool air. I could've breathed him in forever.

At this moment, I needed to gather myself. I had flown apart in his arms and come all over his fingers. I hadn't even meant to kiss him. In fact, I'd been telling myself for days that I shouldn't kiss him again. Somehow, I knew it was risky, more risky than anything for me, for my heart, for the vulnerability I kept hidden away.

I was no fragile flower. I'd been honed and burned and strengthened in the fire of what I had watched my mother go through. I had promised myself I would never be vulnerable to any man. I treated sex like a transaction. I gave men something, and they gave me something in return. Of course, the exchange of sexual favors wasn't particularly equal. Orgasms were rarely part of the exchange for me. I usually had to take care of that myself.

I had no clue how much time had passed since

Cooper had helped me carry groceries into my apartment. It could've been hours, but I suspected it had only been a matter of minutes. The force of my climax left me shaking. There were still little aftershocks echoing through my body.

I felt safe and protected, held against him with his fingers still buried inside me. His other arm wrapped around me, holding me close. He was strong. I could feel the muscles in his arms, the planes of his chest, and the hard, hot length of his arousal against my thigh.

A distant corner of my mind tried to nudge through my awareness, telling me I should take care of him. But it didn't feel right. I sensed he didn't want that, which confused me and made me feel even more vulnerable.

I found power in giving a man pleasure. It was vulnerable to let myself go and be the only one who found pleasure. As much as I tried to collect myself and find some sense of a casual attitude, some sense of distance, it was a struggle.

I finally forced myself to lift my head. I took a shaky breath and braved a look at his face. Cooper's cognac gaze met mine. Seeing that he looked as shocked as I felt, I found just a hint of comfort.

A moment later, his fingers were no longer buried inside me. He tugged my leggings back into place and buttoned the last button on my blouse. I sat on the kitchen counter, my body sated with pleasure still spinning in little eddies inside.

I didn't know what to say, but I had to say something. It wasn't like I was never going to see him again. He lived across the hall. Willow Brook was a tiny town, like a little snow globe in winter, the world contained in a small circle.

I took a breath, wondering just what to say. He lifted his hand and smoothed my hair away from my cheek, tucking it behind my ear. Even though I'd just had an explosive climax, that subtle sensation of his fingers brushing against the shell of my ear and down along the side of my neck before his hand fell away sent another shiver chasing through me.

"I don't do relationships," he said. "I don't mean that to be harsh."

When I searched his eyes, I saw a flicker of vulnerability and some kind of pain under everything. Somebody hurt this man. I wanted to hunt them down and hurt them on his behalf to assuage his pain. Because maybe I didn't know Cooper all that well yet—even though he had just given me the best orgasm of my life —but I knew he was a good man.

He couldn't know it, but he'd just handed me a gift, something that helped me find a way out of my own vulnerability at this moment. "I don't either, so it's okay. Don't worry. Even if I see you every day, this doesn't have to be awkward. Maybe we can give each other what we need."

He angled his head to the side, his eyes narrowing in consideration. I sensed he wanted to say something more but appeared to think better of it. His tongue pressed into the side of his cheek before he nodded. "Maybe we can."

Chapter Thirteen

FARRAH

I didn't see Cooper for a few days. Even though I wanted to see him every day. I was impatient for more, impatient to see what might happen next. Yet not seeing him for a few days was probably for the best. That gave us both a chance to get back on a firm footing of remembering this thing between us didn't have to mean anything. It could be just some fun sexy times.

As autumn approached, the air in Alaska cooled. A burst of fireweed bloomed, a plentiful and stunningly beautiful weed that left the landscape awash in bright fields of fuchsia.

A bunny bounced across the reception counter. "Dragon," the little girl said.

I had to fight back my laughter at the name bestowed upon this gray bunny with floppy ears who looked absolutely nothing like a dragon.

"Is he going to be okay?" she asked, her wide brown eyes peering up at me.

Alice stood in the doorway to the back hall and glanced over when she heard the little girl's question.

"Dragon will be just fine. He had a hairball, and it's all taken care of."

The little girl let out a dramatic sigh of relief. Meanwhile, Dragon nosed the lid on the jar of treats I kept on the counter.

Alice walked over, uncurling her palm and handing the little girl several pieces of lettuce. "This is better than the dog treats," she offered with a smile.

While the little girl fed Dragon his lettuce, I checked the family out, watching Dragon and his owners disappear through the doorway a moment later.

I was making a few adjustments in our payment portal when the bell chimed on the door. I glanced up to see Mae Townsend walk in. She smiled as her cat eyed me suspiciously from the carrier she held.

"Hey there." With a smile, I stood and rounded the desk.

I greeted her cat, Sassafras, with a treat through the carrier's grated door. Mae gave me a quick hug and stepped back. I had gotten to know Mae through Alice and Tiffany. Returning to the back of the desk, I tapped the calendar. "Oh, that's right. Sassafras is scheduled for her annual appointment today."

Mae nodded. "As soon as I put her in the carrier, she gave me *that* look." She gestured to the carrier, where Sassafras gave both of us a haughty glare. "She's not thrilled about this appointment."

I chuckled. "It'll be fine. Alice is always good at keeping pets calm. She's finishing up another appointment," I added. "She's running a little behind. It's been a busy day."

After she set the carrier on the floor in a patch of sunlight cast through the windows, Mae leaned her elbows on the counter. "I'm so glad Alice has gotten this clinic up and running smoothly again. They were never closed, but not having a regular vet meant the schedule was hit or miss."

"I know. It's worked out really well. Let's go on back, and I'll get everything started. I was just out here because Tiffany—" I paused just as the hallway door opened.

"Is here!" Tiffany announced with a flourish as she smiled at Mae and me. "I was running late because I forgot that Ross started basketball today after school. I had to drive back to the house and get his clothes for practice. I'm late, but I'm here now. You all just go on back." She literally shooed me out from behind her desk.

I glanced over at Mae and winked. "Tiffany's kind of territorial about her desk," I whispered loudly with a grin.

Mae snorted. "Understood."

"Thanks for covering," Tiffany called as we walked through the doorway into the hall.

I prepared the shots for when Alice came in to perform Sassafras's annual exam. "How are things going?" I asked as I worked.

Mae stroked her hand between Sassafras's ears through the now open door to the carrier. "Pretty good. I heard you have a new neighbor." She waggled her eyebrows.

"I do. Shocker, he's a hotshot firefighter," I said dryly. "There's a surplus in town."

"No kidding. I meet more firefighters here than I've met anywhere. Cooper is nice," she added.

Oh, the questions I had about Cooper! I was trying my damnedest not to dwell on him, but it was an utter failure. He lived across the hall, and he'd kissed me. I'd come all over his fingers. He crowded my thoughts, bumping everything else out of the way.

Me, cynical me, was thinking, maybe I should have some sort of, maybe not a fling, but an *arrangement* of sorts with him. Yet I knew that was a laughably bad idea. Because Cooper made me want things I'd *never* wanted, and that was treacherous for my heart and most certainly my sanity.

"Farrah?" Mae prompted as my thoughts so easily detoured back to all things Cooper.

"He seems nice," I agreed, glad I had something to focus on as I drew up another shot. "I think Sassafras is due for her rabies shot," I murmured to myself as I scanned her chart on the computer screen.

"I think so," Mae said. "Rowan is hoping Cooper stays in Alaska now that he's here." To my chagrin, she shifted the topic right back to Cooper.

I glanced over at her. "Oh?" I aimed to keep my tone casual.

"Rowan is from North Carolina too, you know?"

I nodded. "Uh-huh."

I'd met Rowan, so I knew he had a Southern accent, but I hadn't put two and two together. "Cooper's from Stolen Hearts Valley too?"

"Yep. Remy let him know about the opening here. His ex screwed around with his best friend." Mae shook her head, closing her eyes before letting out a huff. "There's cheating, and then there's that."

"Oh my God," I breathed. "That is awful."

Mae nodded vigorously. "Seriously. Even worse, his dad recently died, and I guess they were really close. Her excuse was that Cooper wasn't emotionally available for her because he was grieving too much after his dad died."

"Karma will catch up. Sometimes it takes forever."

Mae shrugged. "If she lived here, we would shun her."

My heart ached for Cooper. Maybe I didn't know him that well yet, but I knew, without a doubt, that he was a decent and good man, a good friend, and definitely loyal. Before I could ask further questions, which was probably for the best, Alice popped into the room.

"Hey there!" She leaned down by the table to greet Sassafras in the carrier.

I was relieved for the interruption. I wanted to be nosy about Cooper and ask *all* the questions, but if I got too inquisitive, it might reveal that I *totally* had a thing for him.

Later that evening, I once again dropped my groceries on the floor in the hallway. This time, Cooper didn't appear. I ignored my disappointment. A little while later, there was a light knock on my door. I eyed it curiously. I didn't usually get drop-in visits.

When I opened the door, my pulse lunged. Cooper stood with an envelope in one hand. His eyes were warm when I smiled up at him. My hormones were downright gleeful at his appearance with my belly spinning in flips and heat blazing through me.

"I got your mail," he said simply.

"Oh," I managed.

He handed me the envelope, and our fingers brushed as I took it from him. Little sparks leaped across the surface of my skin from that subtle touch, and I felt breathless.

"Thank you," I belatedly said.

"Of course."

I felt flustered and uncertain of what to do. I wanted to invite him in. But I didn't know if he would want to come in. My hesitation got the best of me.

Just then, he gestured beyond my shoulder. "Something's boiling on your stove."

"Oh!" I spun around. "Thank you again!" I called over my shoulder.

As I dashed from the door into my kitchen, I heard the door click shut behind me.

I turned back, wanting to call out and ask him to stay. But I didn't.

COOPER

"Mom, I'm not calling Cindy," I said, ignoring the frustration rising inside.

I could hear my mother's soft sigh filter through my phone. "Coop, what would it hurt?"

Very few people called me Coop, but my mother was one of them. Every time she used that shortened version of my name, I experienced a pang in my chest. My father had frequently called me that. I missed him. His loss still hurt, although the sharpness of my grief had softened.

He'd been gone over two years now. While I had adjusted to the loss, sometimes, the pain of missing him came out of nowhere and hit me so hard it sucked the air right out of my lungs. Mostly, I was learning to live with it. I knew I was blessed. I had two parents I loved, and my father and I had been really close. He had made me the man I was. Even though he was gone, I would always have that.

"Cindy just wants to apologize," my mother pressed.

"Mom, she's already apologized. I've already

accepted her apology. Forgiveness doesn't mean I'm going to be stupid enough to get back together with her. That's what she wants. You're not saying it, but I can get the idea."

My mother *really* wanted to fix what had happened. Cindy, my former fiancée, was the daughter of one of my mother's friends. My mother liked things to be smooth. She claimed to understand why I didn't want to get back with Cindy, and she'd been understandably upset by Cindy's and Dan's actions, but she still wanted to fix it all.

I wasn't walking around harboring much anger at Cindy. Oh, it still stung. The humiliation was the worst part, but I had let it go. A part of letting it go was knowing that I wasn't going back.

I might never admit it to anyone, but in an odd way, Dan's betrayal had hurt worse. I should've been surprised at what he did, but sadly, I wasn't. He had been my friend since elementary school. He'd always been a little less serious than me, a little more casual about everything. He'd been quick to look for any shortcut he could find in life. He'd usually dated casually, declaring he'd settle down only when he felt like it. His lackadaisical approach to life had been amusing, until it wasn't.

"Mom," I began, marshaling my thoughts. "I know Cindy feels bad about what happened. I know Brenda wants it all to go back the way it was. It's not happening, and she'll have to accept that."

My mother let out a sigh. "I understand, Cooper. I do. I think her mom believes if you would somehow come back and get back together with Cindy, it would fix the whole mess she made."

"Mom, Cindy made the mess, and you should stop feeling bad for her about it. She screwed around with

Dan. I know she hates that people in town know. But plenty of people knew about her and Dan before I did. I can't fix that. Eventually, the gossip will burn out, and people will forget about it. In the meantime, I've moved on."

"Are you seeing someone?"

The lilt of Mother's voice at the end meant she would be more excited about that than me getting back with Cindy. At this point, she just wanted me to fall in love with someone. She'd thought Cindy and I would be like her and my dad—high school sweethearts who made it. She and my dad had been one of those couples—best friends, they'd fallen in love and stayed in love. Until my dad passed away from complications of the heart issues he'd had his whole life.

My mother had been devastated and was still grieving, but she also knew how lucky she'd been. Not everyone got to have the kind of marriage she and my father had. She wanted something like that for me.

I didn't have the heart to tell her I never planned to fall in love. I wasn't swearing off marriage, but it would not be what my parents had.

"Not at the moment, Mom."

My mind flashed to the feel of Farrah pressed against me and my fingers buried inside her. My thoughts skipped tracks to overhearing what she said about her stepfather and that sense of protectiveness flared inside yet again.

"Well, I have faith you'll find someone. In the meantime, I'll just tell Cindy that she'll have to live with the apology she's already made."

"Mom, to clarify, when I come to visit Stolen Hearts Valley, if I see Cindy, we'll talk. But I'm not bending to her will and giving her another chance to badger me. It's exhausting. She made her choices and will have to live with the consequences. Speaking of visits, you said you wanted to come to Alaska. I'm thinking maybe you should try to get here before it gets too cold."

"I was just looking at flights," my mother replied. "Rowan's mother wants to travel with me. We talked the other day and could travel there in two weeks. That's why I was calling. I got sidetracked. I should be able to stay for two weeks. Rowan's wife, Mae, arranged for us to stay in a nearby guesthouse, so I won't even impose on you."

I chuckled. I had warned my mother that I had a one-bedroom apartment. I would've gladly let her use my bedroom while I slept on the couch, but she would've felt bad about displacing me like that.

"Mom, that's great. I'm glad you'll have company on the flight. It's not a short one."

"From when we get on the plane here until we land in Anchorage, it will be fifteen hours! I could fly to Europe faster than that."

"I know. Mom, I gotta roll," I said, glancing at the clock on the wall in the break area in the back of the fire station.

"Of course. I love you."

"Love you too, Mom."

I ended the call, tossing my phone on the table and reaching for my coffee. I took a bracing swallow. I *would* be glad to see my mom. I missed her. I'd had mixed feelings about taking this job in Alaska when the opportunity came up, yet my mom had wanted me to go. She was still grieving my father, but she had a lot of friends. She wasn't a wealthy woman, but she and my father had planned wisely, so their house had been paid off years before my father passed away. She lived comfortably and assured me that while she would always miss my father, she kept herself busy.

I contemplated her comments about Cindy. My mom was a pleaser. She wanted everyone to be happy. Even though she'd been furious about what Cindy did, she was still friends with Cindy's mom, and I knew that was a source of pressure for her. Stolen Hearts Valley was a small town, just like Willow Brook. In any small town, it was hard to escape rumors. Nobody would argue that someone screwing around with their fiancé's friend was a good look. I was thoroughly over Cindy, but Dan's involvement still burned.

When it came to having a good time, Dan put himself first. He was a funny guy, always good for a laugh and a little fun. The problem was, he usually got away with a lot, and people cut him a lot of slack as a result. To this day, I think he thought we could somehow rebuild those bridges. I could be friendly, but I could never be the guy he called when he needed something. Not anymore.

"What's up?" Beck asked, his voice snapping through my thoughts. He'd just walked out of the locker room with damp hair from a recent shower. During lulls between fires out in the backcountry, we did training exercises and so on here at the station. He poured a cup of coffee and sat down across from me, eyeing me expectantly.

I shrugged. "Not much."

Just then, Rowan appeared through that same doorway. "Just got off the phone with my mom," he began as he mirrored Beck's actions, pouring a cup of coffee and sitting down. "I guess my mom and your mom are traveling here together." He flashed a grin. "I gotta say, I'm relieved. It's nice my mom will have someone with her. Mae and I love having her visit, but..." He shrugged.

"I get it. I don't really have space for company. I have a nice apartment, but I'd have to give up my bed for my mom. I have no problem doing that, but this way, she'll be hanging out with your mom. They can hit the town together."

Beck glanced at us both. "I'll give them my mom's number. Maybe they can have a night on the town together."

"We'll send them to the Gallery Café, though, not Wildlands," Rowan deadpanned.

We laughed together. I took another swallow of coffee just as Rowan said, "So my mom tells me your mom hopes you and Cindy work things out."

I sputtered on my coffee, managing not to make a mess. I lowered my cup and cleared my throat. "Fuck my life," I muttered. "My mom just talked to me about it. I guess Cindy is sad about how things turned out." I let out a sigh as I scrubbed a hand over my hair.

"Who is Cindy? And what did she do?" Beck asked.

I slid my gaze to him. "Anybody ever point out you're nosy?"

Unabashed, Beck nodded. "I'm nosy as fuck. But if you tell me to keep something quiet, I will." He crossed his hand over his heart.

Rowan snorted. "He will. Sorry, maybe I shouldn't have mentioned it."

I shrugged. "Cindy is my ex-fiancée. She screwed around with a good friend of mine back in my home-town, so I broke things off."

Those were the bare bones of the situation. I left out her excuse about how I'd been emotionally unavailable because I was grieving too much after my dad died. What the ever-loving fuck? Talk about a situation that offered the opportunity to see what someone might do when the chips were down. I was relieved I'd learned that about Cindy before we got married.

Beck narrowed his eyes. "Your ex screwed around with your friend?"

"Yup," I said dryly.

"Some people never learn," he returned.

"Never learn what?" Rowan prompted.

"That there are always consequences. I'm not the kind of guy who believes life is here to punish us, and I'm not a big fan of carrying the shame and guilt and shit forever. Because we all fuck up. Maybe she really feels bad. Maybe your friend really feels bad, or he's not really your friend," he corrected. "But what the hell? Did she think you were gonna just go back and make nice in a small town, knowing she already fucked around with one of your friends?"

I nodded in agreement. "I'm with you there." For all his nosiness and teasing, Beck was a solid guy with his head screwed on straight. Maybe it was being a dad, perhaps it was life, but he seemed to know his priorities. "I told my mom to stop feeling bad for Cindy." Glancing at Rowan, I added, "You know her. She always wants to please everybody. I don't need to hear all the details to know that Cindy is embarrassed. It's been over a year, but it is a small town. She can't really run from those rumors. I'm not refusing to get back together with her because I refused to forgive her. I've honestly forgiven her. I'm not mad, not anymore, but I'm over her. She showed me how she handles life when hard things happen. Hopefully, she learns from it so when she falls in love again, if she does, she'll handle it differently."

A few hours later, I was home. It was dark outside,

and I didn't know where Humpty was. When I got home, I realized I had left the bathroom window open, not too much, but wide enough for a cat to knock the screen loose and slip out.

I was seriously worried. My first fear had been that Humpty died jumping out the second-story window. But there was no sign of him outside. I hoped cats really had nine lives, and hopefully, he had eight lives left.

I immediately called Wes. "Can a cat survive a jump from a second-story window?"

"Probably," Wes replied, sounding way too calm. "Did he jump out a window?"

"I think so," I grumbled. "There's no sign of him on the ground outside the window."

"Put some food outside."

"I will. I'll call you when I find him." I was seriously worried because I'd only had this cat for two months. I loved the little guy.

I grabbed my jacket and my keys, along with a small bag of his favorite soft treats, before walking outside. I'd never gone looking for a runaway cat before, so I had no idea where to start. I just kept calling his name and ringing the little bell on the catnip toy that Farrah had gifted him when she took care of him.

Chapter Fifteen

FARRAH

"Are we all locked up?" Alice called from the hallway.

I was literally flipping the bolt on the front door to the vet clinic when I turned around to find her standing in the doorway to the hall.

Lifting the keys, I gave them a little jingle. "All locked up."

As I slipped into my jacket, Alice asked, "Do you want to swing by Wildlands and grab a drink?"

I glanced over. "I'm meeting my mom for dinner, so rain check?"

"Maybe tomorrow?" Tiffany prompted when she appeared behind Alice in the hallway.

"Let's plan on it."

We walked out together, and a few minutes later, I was driving the short distance from the vet clinic down Main Street to the Gallery Café. When I passed Willow Brook Fire & Rescue, my eyes shifted to the back parking area. I didn't even want to admit I was searching for Cooper's truck. I knew exactly what he drove because he usually parked his truck beside mine behind the building where we lived.

"You're being ridiculous," I whispered to myself.

I didn't need to wonder where Cooper was. He wasn't my first neighbor. I'd been living in that little apartment for over six months now. The last person had been some guy who worked in commercial fishing. He'd told me he'd be leaving when fishing season was over. He'd been friendly, even handsome, but I had never once felt my pulse race at the sound of his footsteps in the hallway or peered out my window into the parking area to see if he was home.

This crush on Cooper was getting out of control, and I needed to get over it. I told myself it was a good thing I was having dinner with my mom. I would be occupied. I wouldn't be wondering if he would have some reason to knock on my door and kiss me and make me come all over his fingers again. Better yet, I would have no reason to wonder if maybe some kind of friends-with-benefits arrangement would be the best thing ever. I wanted more, so much more.

Ordering my brain to stop obsessing over Cooper, I turned into the parking area at the Gallery Café. This was an art gallery with an attached restaurant that showcased rotating displays of artwork. The food was excellent, and they had theme weeks for the restaurant. This week's theme was Italian. I was a sucker for good Italian food. Load me up with carbs and sauces and cheese, and I was in heaven. I didn't care what anyone said about carbs. I refused to start counting them. What the actual fuck?

When I walked inside, my mother was already there. The place she lived with her friend was just down the street, so she usually walked if we met here. She smiled as soon as she saw me, approaching and folding me into a quick hug. "Hi, sweetie," she said as she stepped back.

"Hey, Mom." My lips curled into a smile.

I liked that we were both making an effort to foster our relationship, but it was an odd feeling, like new shoes that were stiff when you hoped they'd get comfortable soon. Dinner out with just my mom *never* happened when my stepfather was alive. We didn't really have any kind of relationship independent from him. She lived under the weight of his near-constant control and disapproval, and that was the way it had been.

Before we could say anything further, the host appeared. "Right this way," he said, gesturing with his hand. As we were walking through the gallery area, I saw another friend, Jasmine Ryan, talking with a couple looking at her pottery. She helped run the gallery and had her own pottery shown here. I waved, getting a smile and a return wave.

After we were seated and had ordered, I glanced over at my mother. I still experienced pangs of guilt when I thought about the relief I felt at her finally being free from Gerald and the life she'd been trapped in with him.

Dinner went as dinner had been going with my mother lately. We chatted about superficial things and managed to avoid the fraught topics. We were sharing a dessert, and I sensed she was nervous about something. Trepidation slipped through me.

After a bite, she took a swallow of water, studying me. "Your grandparents asked me how you're doing."

"Excuse me?" I prompted, legitimately confused.

My father's parents had been barely in my life before they passed away, and my mother ended up estranged from her parents after my stepfather had a huge argument with my grandfather.

"My parents," she said softly.

"Oh, *oh*. When did you hear from them?"

This was one of those landmine topics. After my stepfather had basically banished them from our lives, we never heard from them. I didn't even know how to reach them.

My mother took another swallow of water. When she lowered her glass, she traced her fingertip along the side of it, the motion restless. "I reached out. Told them Gerald died." She cleared her throat. "They'd love to see you."

My heart pounded in an unsteady beat, a painful, unsettling ache in my chest like a cold ball. I took a breath, setting my fork down, and reaching for my napkin. After dabbing at my mouth, I twisted the napkin nervously in my fingers. "Where are they?"

"They never moved. Dad had a stroke, but he's okay."

Anger jolted me briefly. Over the years, I sometimes wondered if I had subconsciously trained my anger to pass through me swiftly. Anger wasn't a safe emotion to have when my stepfather was alive. I couldn't act on it, and it was futile.

"Mom, why did you let Gerald cut them off? I'm not even asking for myself, but for you. I don't understand."

My mother's face was pale. For a moment, it almost felt as if the ghost of my stepfather—if that was even possible—hung in the air between us. The look on her face was so painfully familiar. There was a blankness to her expression, a careful control where all emotion was wiped away. There could be nothing to misinterpret, nothing to react to, nothing to elicit any guessing or wondering. Just nothing. Just blank. That nothingness represented so much for me.

My anger rose again, like the roar of a lion inside

my chest. I clenched the napkin in my fingers. "Don't look at me like that. You're allowed to have a feeling, Mom," I said, my voice low, vibrating with pent-up anger tangled with sadness, resentment, and helplessness. Because I couldn't fix anything that had happened before. Not at all.

My mother's lips pressed together, and she took in a slow breath, her nostrils flaring. "I know. I didn't know how to get out. If I could change it, I would. Gerald threatened to kill me if I left. He told me he would win custody in court even though he was only your stepfather. You know how much money his family had. He was a lawyer; his father was a lawyer. You know he could've made life a living hell for both of us. Worse than it was to live with him. I didn't ever want that to happen." She blinked quickly, and I saw a tear slide out of the corner of one eye.

Abruptly, I felt terribly guilty for even asking. "Mom," I began. "You don't have to—"

She shook her head swiftly. "I do." Her voice was stronger this time, and color was returning to her cheeks. "I would've died to protect you, but I didn't know what would happen to you if I tried to leave and something happened to me. Sometimes I wanted to die. I don't know how to explain it. Maybe it doesn't make sense unless you experience something like it. It didn't start that way with him."

I had seen pictures of them when they started dating. Maybe we hadn't talked about it at length, but my mom had looked happy in those pictures. It had been a whirlwind courtship. They'd been married within months of meeting.

I knew how Gerald could come across. He was a lawyer from a family with money. He was *that* guy, the one who could sweet-talk anyone. I'd heard whispered threats from him when he told her no one would believe her. He rarely, very rarely, used physical violence. Instead, it was the pressure of his emotional manipulation, his constant berating of her, and the ever-present threat he might raise the stakes. I imagined it was like living with a venomous snake always poised to strike. It was unfair to snakes to even compare them. Snakes were just snaking. Gerald was a broken, cruel man.

"He told me he would win custody if I tried to leave. As awful as it was, I preferred he target me rather than you, so it seemed better to stay."

"He would've," I whispered, that old sense of defeat rising like a tired wave. I let out a soft sigh.

She nodded, just once. "I couldn't protect you from him, but I tried to protect you from the worst of it. I'm sorry, more sorry than you'll ever know."

"I'm glad he's dead," I said the words that had dogged me for two whole years. "Are you?"

She cocked her head to the side. "Glad isn't the word. A part of me is relieved, and a part of me is sad. No one is all good or bad. I'm relieved not to have—" She moved her hand quickly back and forth in the air. "All of the awful. I don't even know how else to describe it. But sometimes Gerald could be good. If I'm being honest, I suppose, more than anything, I'm relieved. I wish I could fix it and make it so it didn't affect you."

She studied me for a quiet moment, and I took a swallow of water. My hands were actually shaking. After I set my glass down, I tucked them on my lap under the table and shook them, trying to discharge the unsteady energy cycling through me.

"I worry that you're cynical about relationships," she said gently.

"You don't need to worry." My voice was clear even through the static of discomfort I felt inside. "I am cynical, and I like it that way. When I was in college before I did my vet tech training, I took a class on gender and violence, and they had a whole section on the frequency of violence against women. It's wildly common. The odds are against me finding a good man. Not just me, but most women. It's the world we live in. It was good to learn that it wasn't just us. It wasn't just you. I don't need a man. I don't ever intend to fall in love. I can't imagine it happening, and that's for the best." My voice had risen to the point of sounding shrill.

I paused. A sense of defensiveness flared inside when I saw the look in my mother's eyes. She felt sad for me. "Be honest with yourself, Mom. You're not going to date again." My angry tone dared her to contradict me.

Her lips twisted to the side as she let out a sigh. "No, I'm not. I don't really want to worry about it. I like living with my friend and not worrying about men. If I can scrape the money together, I'm going to fly your grandparents up here, or I'll go down to see them. I thought they might like the trip, though. What do you think?"

I resisted the urge to point out that she never had to lose so many years with her parents. But I also understood why she stayed. It wasn't safe. Pushing back against my stepfather only led to more misery.

"I'd love to see them. Is travel okay for Grandad?"

My mother nodded quickly. "Yes. Mom said he recovered almost fully from his stroke. They said they'd love to see Alaska."

"I'll help pay for any travel."

She didn't get much of anything after my stepfather died. He spent excessively even though he made good money. Because he was a stingy, vengeful asshole, he had refused to get a life insurance policy for her. His family was as unhelpful and hateful as he had been. All she had was his Social Security benefits. She'd quit working when they married because he'd told her she didn't need to work. I viewed that as yet another way to limit her world, her contact with others.

"That would be nice," she said softly. "I don't want to rely on you, though."

"Mom, I want to help. I tell you all the time that my bills aren't that much. I make decent money. If you need something, I'll help."

When I drove away after dinner, I felt unsettled. That conversation with my mother had hurt. Even though he was dead, it scared me to think that Gerald threatened to kill her if she ever tried to leave. Yet intellectually, I knew that threat was genuine. That class taught me the most dangerous time for a woman in an abusive relationship was when she tried to leave.

As unsettled as I felt, these conversations with my mother were a victory. This topic had been so firmly off-limits for so long that, in a way, it felt like a big fuck you to my stepfather to even talk about it.

"Fuck you," I said loudly in the car. "Fuck you, Gerald."

I didn't even notice I'd been crying until I felt the tears cooling as they slid down my cheeks.

After I climbed out of my car, I slipped my keys into my purse and started to walk around to the entrance when I heard Cooper's voice calling, "Humpty, here! Humpty Dumpty!" This was followed by a little bell jingling.

Chapter Sixteen

FARRAH

"Cooper!" I called into the darkness.

A few seconds later, footsteps approached. "Hey!" he called as he exited the trees on the back side of the parking lot.

"Is Humpty lost?" We met at the edge of the parking area where the glow from the lights by the building entrance reached.

He wore a worried expression as he looked down at me and nodded. "Yes." He ran a hand through his hair. "I forgot to close my bathroom window. You know it's one of those crank windows?"

I nodded. "Yeah, I have the same one."

"Well, when I got home, the screen was pushed out. I don't know where he is. I was worried maybe he died jumping out. But when I called Wes, he said a cat could survive a jump like that."

Together, we looked up to the back window in question.

"Oh yeah, he probably survived. And if he didn't—"

Cooper interjected, "I would've found him on the ground. Have you ever found a lost cat?"

"Absolutely." I nodded firmly. "We need to put food out by the door, but let's keep looking now." I eyed the trees behind the building. "He's probably right back there. He's neutered, so I doubt he wandered far. Plus, he's old, and he likes his comfort." I reached over, lightly squeezing Cooper's upper arm to comfort him.

Cooper smiled ruefully. "I hope so. You don't have to help me find him."

"I want to help." I was honestly relieved to have a distraction.

We walked into the trees together. Although we were in downtown Willow Brook, it wasn't crowded by any stretch. The small wooded area behind the apartment building was maybe an acre with another street behind it.

The leaves crunched under our feet with autumn upon us. Cooper jingled the small bell attached to the mouse stuffed with catnip that I had given him for Humpty last week.

"I think I need to get some more catnip stuffed animals," Cooper said through the darkness.

"Oh yeah?"

"He loves them, even if he destroys them."

I smiled over at Cooper even though he couldn't see me. "I'll get him some."

"I think you're kind of like his favorite grandmother with the presents," he said dryly.

"His grandmother!" I exclaimed.

"Okay, I didn't mean to imply that you seemed old. But you spoil him and take care of him when I need help."

I snorted. "Good catch."

I wanted to reach over and hold Cooper's hand,

and for God's sake, that was weird. I wasn't a hand holding kind of girl. That was the kind of thing people did when they were a couple. We were *not* a couple. I didn't do couple-y things.

Just then, we heard some rustling nearby. We both stopped. Reflexively, I reached my hand over only to find Cooper reaching for mine. I squeezed once his fingers were laced with mine, whispering, "Maybe that's him."

We stood in complete silence as we waited. My heart pounded in anticipation of the hope that this was Humpty and startled at how good it felt to have Cooper's hand grasping mine. His palm was warm and dry and strong. The link to him felt good. I wanted to step a little closer.

The rustling had stopped. I was about to tell Cooper to jingle the bell, but he did it anyway. A second later, we heard a distinct meow.

"Humpty!" I called. "Humpty!"

A moment later, we heard another meow, and we could see Humpty approaching us. Cooper lifted his phone, turning on the flashlight as I leaned down, releasing Cooper's hand to scoop up Humpty.

"Oh, my goodness! You're all wet!" Humpty was very wet and appeared to be covered in some kind of slime, which was now all over me.

"Do you want me to take him?" Cooper asked as he scanned the light over Humpty in my arms, careful not to shine it into his face.

"No need to take him. I'm already covered in whatever's on him," I said, wishing I'd thought to zip my jacket up. I could feel the moisture seeping through the thin cotton of my shirt.

Humpty let out a plaintive meow. Cooper lowered the flashlight, scratching on the top of his head, the only part of his body that appeared even a tiny bit clean.

"There's a culvert between the parking area for our building and Firehouse Café. He must've gotten wet in there."

"Did you go for a swim?" Cooper asked Humpty as we turned and began walking through the trees toward the parking area.

"He's shivering," I commented, holding the cat a little closer against me and pulling one side of my jacket around his body.

A few minutes later, we were walking up the stairs. "Humpty." I looked down at him when we crested the top of the stairs. "You stink." His shivering was starting to slow.

Cooper unlocked his door, gesturing me inside his apartment. I looked up at him. "We should just take him straight over to the kitchen sink and give him a bath. I shouldn't even put him on the floor. Because if I do, this—" I gestured down at Humpty's body. I wrinkled my nose as I looked back up at Cooper. "Slimy, wet, and stinky stuff will get everywhere."

Cooper chuckled. "I'm so sorry."

"Don't worry. I'll change later. For now, go turn on your hot water."

"I don't have cat bath soap," he added as he shut the door quickly and crossed over to the kitchen. He shrugged out of his jacket and tossed it on the counter with his keys. Seconds later, he had the hot water running.

I knew I was going to have to wash my shirt and my jacket, really everything I was wearing, so I just followed him over. "We can just use dish soap. We have to go with what we have at this point. Once I get him in there, go grab a towel. The dish towels won't be enough to dry him off."

Humpty appeared to realize what was about to happen when I stopped beside the kitchen sink because he began wiggling in my arms. "Oh no, you don't! You escaped today and had quite the adventure, but you're getting clean. You stink and you're filthy."

"Are you sure you don't need help holding him?" Cooper asked doubtfully.

"I'm a vet tech. I can wrangle a cat who doesn't want a bath. Go get the towel and be ready. We're going to do this as fast as we can."

Cooper reached down to close the drain and squirt some soap in the water as it filled the sink. I kept a firm hold on Humpty as I lowered him into the sink.

I moved swiftly, soaping him, then running the warm water over him before lifting the drain to rinse him. Cooper had returned quickly with a towel. When I was satisfied all of Humpty was clean, I turned the water off and ran my hands over his fur to swipe as much moisture off as I could.

I glanced up at Cooper, who was standing right beside me. "He's not happy with me," I offered. "But instead of freaking out and scratching or biting me, he's taking the stoic approach."

We looked down at Humpty together. He sat in the sink with my arm wrapped firmly around his body. He looked downright disgusted at the entire situation.

"If you hadn't broken out and run away and gotten wet and muddy and gross, none of this would have happened," I explained to him. Humpty wouldn't even look at me.

Cooper helped me dry him off, then we finally let him go. He leaped onto the floor and made a mad dash for the back of the sofa where he eyed me suspiciously.

"You closed the bathroom window, right?" I asked suddenly, looking up at Cooper.

"Oh, absolutely. I closed it when I realized he was gone. No worries. Every window is closed. I checked before I left."

Humpty jumped to the floor and ran in circles around the apartment before hopping back on the couch and rubbing himself all over it. Cooper watched with a slow smile stretching across his face. When I looked up at him, my belly swooped. His eyes met mine, and he grinned. "He's home."

Just then, I remembered I was covered in mud and brown slime and probably smelled something like Humpty. I looked down at myself. "Oh my God. I'm going to have to go downstairs to the laundry room."

"Oh, I have laundry in here," he said quickly.

"You do?" My eyes widened as I glanced back up at him.

"One of the previous tenants installed one of those small stacked washer and dryer sets. You're welcome to use it."

I nodded before I could think better of it. Cooper gestured toward his bathroom door. "All yours."

I hadn't even noticed I still had my purse on my shoulder. In my rush to get Humpty into the sink, I'd forgotten about it. I carefully took it off and set it on the counter.

Cooper watched me, offering, "I'll clean off the strap for you."

Holding my arms out to my sides, I walked over and kicked off my shoes by the door before hurrying into the bathroom. I'd managed to get the stinky slime just about everywhere except for my shoes. I peeled everything off and stuffed them into the washer, seeing Cooper conveniently had the laundry soap on the shelf. Aside from this addition, his bathroom was like mine. A rainfall shower was centered over an oval-shaped tub with a curtain pulled around it. The toilet and sink were to the side. Where I had wider shelving, he had the washer and dryer, with a small set of shelves tucked between them and the door.

I was a little jealous. I made a mental note to ask Janet if I could add one to my bathroom. I hopped in the shower, savoring the hot water. I had Humpty's slime everywhere, even in the ends of my hair.

Chapter Seventeen

FARRAH

It wasn't until I stepped out of the shower and started drying off that I realized all of my clothes were in the washer and I was completely naked. My only option would be to walk out with a towel wrapped around me.

"Oh well. Oh hell," I whispered to myself as I dried off.

I ran my fingers through my hair after rubbing it with a towel to get it sort of dry. I studied myself in the mirror. I was flushed all over from the hot water. I glanced over at the washer, my eyes landing on the digital screen to see that even though I had selected the quick wash option, twenty whole minutes were still left.

I wrapped the fluffy towel around me, securing it tightly above my breasts, and gathered my dignity. When I looked down at my feet just before I opened the door, I laughed to myself. My toenails were painted bright purple, a fun color.

Whatever. It didn't matter what Cooper thought of my toenails. Surely, he would understand that I wouldn't be walking out in a towel unless I waited in the bathroom until my clothes were dry, which would probably be an hour or so.

When I stepped out, he was seated on one of the kitchen stools, looking at something on his phone. I cleared my throat as I crossed the room with one hand curled over the top of the towel where the fabric was tucked in.

"I need to get some clothes," I announced.

Cooper set his phone down, his eyes whipping over to mine. I was already flush from the shower, but heat blazed through me the second our gazes collided. I stopped a few feet away from him and cleared my throat again, shifting on my feet. He simply stared at me, his mouth parting slightly before he closed it quickly.

He thumbed toward the door. "I can—" His hand dropped, and his eyes narrowed. It felt as if the air around us shimmered to life, almost electric. "Come here," he said, his voice low.

I couldn't have stopped myself from responding to his command if I wanted to. The floor was cool under my feet, while the rest of my body was on fire. I took one step, and then another, and another until I stood right in front of him.

He reached for me, one hand coming to rest on my hip. His palm slid from there around my waist to rest just at the base of my spine, where his fingers splayed over the upper curve of my bottom. He coaxed me closer to him with the subtlest of pressure.

I stood between his knees, feeling my heartbeat pounding hard and fast. My breath was short, and I swallowed. His eyes were dark.

"I want you," he rasped.

I tore my eyes from his, looking down. My gaze landed on his muscled thigh, shifting upward to see the hard ridge of his cock visible through his jeans. That sent a rush of arousal through me. I could feel it between my thighs. I shifted on my feet, needing to do something, anything, to relieve the pressure building there.

"Look at me," he commanded.

I lifted my eyes to his again, and the look there nearly took my breath away. My knees felt liquid, and one of my palms fell to his thigh. I needed something to hold me up.

"Tell me what you want," he whispered.

I knew precisely what I wanted—him filling me while I came all over his cock instead of his fingers.

I could still feel the subtle press of his hand, coaxing me closer. He lifted his other hand, the backs of his knuckles trailing across the towel drawn tight over my breasts.

"Tell me what you want," he repeated.

Chapter Eighteen

COOPER

Farrah's green eyes darkened from jade to a deep green, like a shaded forest. Her tongue slid across her bottom lip.

"You," she finally replied.

I could feel the beat of my heart in my cock. I didn't realize I'd been waiting until she spoke. A sense of relief gusted through me. Her hand dropped away from her towel to mold over my cock.

"More, this time," she added. Her palm dragged over the denim, and my cock swelled even further.

I gritted my teeth, sucking in a breath of air. I needed to say something before this spiraled out of control.

"I want more too, but I have to say something first."

Farrah studied me for a few beats. "If you're worried about us being neighbors and crossing paths in this small town, don't. I don't do serious. I don't do relationships."

She said something along the lines of what I was about to say, and I should've been relieved. Yet her direct comments stung a little. Certainty rang in her tone.

I swallowed. "Okay, I won't worry."

She was quiet. Her palm remained on the length of my cock.

I hadn't considered my words and didn't know what I would've said. It would've been something along the lines of, "I believe in romance, but I don't believe in love, so don't count on me for that."

I didn't think I could've said that to her because she made me question my own certainty. I didn't want to think too hard about that just now.

She leaned forward, dropping a hot kiss on the side of my neck just as she dragged her hand up and down. The rush of need made it easy to forget, to think, to wonder why I might question my commitment to *never* being committed. I trailed my knuckles across the upper curves of her breast, just over the towel, before lifting my hand and sliding it into her hair.

One fiery second burned into the next as we stared at each other. On the heels of a breath, we were kissing. Her mouth opened underneath mine, and she let out this soft whimper that I could literally feel inside, a subtle tug of connection, a craving for more. More of Farrah, more of everything with her.

I coaxed her a little closer as my other palm slid up her spine with my fingers curling over the back of the towel. I wanted to rip it off right now. Competing with that urge was my desire to savor every single fucking second of this.

Her tongue tangled with mine as our kiss went deeper. She shifted closer, and I could feel my cock cradled against her hips as her hand fell away, sliding under the hem of my T-shirt, over my abs, and around my waist. Her fingertips pressed into the muscles along my spine.

We finally broke apart, breathing raggedly as we stared at each other. Farrah was impatient, shoving up my shirt. I reached behind my head, catching the fabric in my fist, and yanked it up and over.

She leaned forward and strung kisses across my chest. Each soft kiss sent ripples of heat through me. She dragged her palm over my cock again before yanking at the buttons on my fly. She made a sound of impatience. I shifted slightly, sliding off the stool so my hips were propped against it.

I meant to say something, to take control of the moment, but she was fast. Another fiery second later, her palm slid into the opening where my jeans were undone, shoving them down until my cock bounced free.

"Farrah—" I began.

Her gaze lifted to mine, and she swiped her tongue across her bottom lip, sending electricity sizzling down my spine and another shot of blood straight to my cock.

"Just a minute," she whispered.

She leaned over, curling her palm around my length just as she dropped an open kiss on the tip of my cock. I laced my fingers in her hair, holding on for dear life as she sucked lightly on the crown, her tongue swirling around it before she fully took me in her mouth. A ragged groan escaped, and my fingers tightened in her hair. She drew upward with a subtle suction as her palm followed her mouth up and then down, once, twice, yet again. I was clinging to my control. Usually, I had far more discipline than this, but I was already teetering on the edge of release, my balls tightening and the pressure rapidly building. Her tongue swirled around the crown before she took me in once again.

"Farrah—" I bit out, meaning to tell her to stop, to wait, to give me a minute to breathe.

But it was too late. Once more, she sucked me in, and the pressure snapped. I came in spurts in her mouth, the pleasure indescribable as I clung to her hair and waited for the shudders to slow.

A moment later, she drew back slowly, releasing me with a pop before she straightened. Her lips were puffy, her cheeks flushed pink, and her eyes wide and dark. I was grateful I had something to lean against behind me, or otherwise, my knees would've given out at how raw and sensual she looked.

I took a breath, marshaling some semblance of composure. "Fuck me, Farrah," I muttered gruffly.

Her lips curled at the corners, and the look in her eyes was sly and teasing. "Can you fuck me? Please," she teased.

I took another breath and reached for her, sliding my hand around her waist and coaxing her closer. My other hand slid out of her hair.

I trailed my knuckles along her jawline and over the downy skin of her neck. "I think we should head to the bedroom. The counter's handy, but we've already tested that out."

She grinned. I had enough strength to stand now and caught her hand in mine, leading her from the kitchen into the bedroom. I flicked the light switch on.

This time, I took control, turning to catch her hand again and leading her to the foot of the bed. I lifted her hips onto it and rested my hands on either side of her as I took her mouth in a slow, devouring kiss.

When I lifted my head, she was breathing in sharp little pants, her eyes dark pools of desire, reflecting my own need back to me. I curled my fingers over the top of her towel and gave it a little tug. It loosened, and she waited. One more tug, and it fell in a rumple around her hips.

My breath seized in my lungs as I stared at her for a long, heart-pounding moment. Her skin was still flushed rosy pink from her shower. Her breasts were plump and full, her nipples deep pink and drawn into tight little buds.

I dipped my head, closing my mouth over one nipple with light suction. I grazed my teeth over it before drawing back, savoring her gasp. I teased both of her nipples. She'd buried her hands in my hair, and her hips rocked restlessly.

Only then did I push her back with my palm pressed lightly in the valley between her breasts. I lingered, feeling greedy to touch her silky-soft skin, to tease her, to feel the weight of her breasts in my palms. I dropped hot kisses over her belly, gratified at her pleas.

"Cooper, please!" she gasped.

I was already hard again to the point of pain. I slid a palm up the inside of her thigh and pushed her knee out. Finally, fucking *finally*, I let my eyes drop to her very core. She was pink and slick with arousal. I could see her pretty clit, swollen and pushed out.

I teased my fingers through her folds as her hips rocked into my touch. My mouth watered, and I finally gave in to the fierce need and brought my mouth to her sex. Her hips bucked into me instantly. She was salty, tangy, and sweet. I fucked her with my fingers as I tasted her. All the while, she moaned and shifted restlessly under my attention.

When she pleaded, "Cooper, now!" I finally swirled my tongue over her clit, giving it the lightest suction. She came with a sharp cry while her entire body shuddered.

I stayed with her through it until she went limp and languid. By this point, I needed more. I needed all of her. Clinging to the tiniest bit of restraint, I straightened, kicking my jeans and boxers free. I was just about to stretch out over her and fill her when a distant voice reminded me of the practicalities.

"Fuck," I muttered. Pushing away from the bed, I strode quickly into the bathroom.

I knew right where I had a few condoms. Old habits died hard, so I always kept a few condoms with my toiletries. I quickly found them and tossed the wrapper in the trash, walking back into the bedroom as I rolled it on.

Farrah was waiting, resting on her elbows. She shimmied back on the bed as I approached. The mattress dipped when I placed a knee between her thighs. I stretched out over her. She welcomed me, curling her legs around my hips with her arms sliding around my shoulders as she whispered, "More."

I lifted my head, looking into her eyes as I notched myself at her entrance. "Now?" I rasped.

She bit her lip, nodding as her hips rocked into me. In one deep thrust, I filled her, letting out a slurred moan at the sensation of her slick core rippling around me.

Chapter Nineteen

FARRAH

I tried to catch my breath, but my body was awash in sensation as the echoes of my climax reverberated. And now, with Cooper filling and stretching me, I was already spiraling again. The pressure ratcheted it up inside, need driving me ruthlessly.

He held still as my body adjusted to him. I felt stretched and full. I took a shuddering breath and felt myself begin to relax around him. Dragging my eyes open, I found his gaze waiting, dark and intent.

"Is this okay?" he asked.

I nodded, my hips moving on instinct and rocking slightly toward him. He drew back, and I cried out when he filled me again. Pleasure spun through me at the delicious slide. He rested on his elbows, watching me as he moved in slow thrusts, taking his sweet time and not rushing, not even a little. Yet the slowness itself was like being caught in a fiery dream. Each notch deeper into me sent pleasure spinning tighter and tighter inside. I was sensitive from my last climax. He angled his hips just so, so that with every subtle thrust into me, he created friction over my swollen clit.

I held on tight with my palms pressing into his spine, feeling the flexion as we rocked together. I couldn't look away, caught in his eyes, in this burning-hot dream of pleasure and need.

Everything spun as pressure built with each thrust. I was panting his name when Cooper shifted, a palm dragging down over my belly. His fingers teased exactly where I needed his touch. My climax came in a rush. Wave after wave after wave, I felt pleasure breaking through me. I distantly heard myself moaning and crying his name.

I felt him follow me over the edge. All of his muscles went taut as he trembled above me. I could barely think. I was breathing in desperate gulps of air as he eased down over me before rolling over until I was resting half on top of him. We lay still together, breathing in ragged pants.

I rested against Cooper, the rush of sensations swirling through me beginning to slow, like waves lapping against the shore as the tide rolled out. As my mind slowly flickered back into awareness, I began to panic in a corner of my thoughts. I wasn't supposed to feel this way.

It was usually easy to keep my distance. So easy that I didn't even have to try. Just now, I felt as if I had been walking through a forest and unexpectedly came upon the edge of a cliff. And now, I scrambled to back away from the edge, stumbling and losing my balance.

I told myself I should roll away from him. I should get my towel and walk across the hallway into my own apartment, where I would fall asleep by myself.

I stayed where I was.

Chapter Twenty

FARRAH

I felt the warmth of a palm resting in the curve of my waist, an arm curling around my back. I burrowed closer, savoring the feeling of warmth, of being held, of being protected and safe.

My eyes flew open. The room was dark. I could feel the steady beat of Cooper's heart under my palm where it rested slightly off-center on his chest, along the edge of his rib cage.

His breathing was slow and even. Meanwhile, I had gone from a state of utter restfulness to teetering on the edge of anxiety-fueled distress.

I had *never*, not even once, fallen asleep with a man. With anyone, for that matter.

My heart beat as fast as a jackrabbit in my chest. I was too panicked to move. I feared any motion would wake Cooper. I *definitely* didn't want to do that. Lord knows that might mean conversation, and I was a hot mess, in the middle of the night just from waking up.

I forced myself to take slow and deep breaths, and my pulse gradually began to dial down. Cooper was warm and all muscle-y. I snuggled up against him like a little barnacle with one leg hooked over his, my body plastered to his side, and my arm curled over him. His hold was relaxed and secure.

When my anxiety began to abate, I opened my eyes again. A soft light emanated from outside his bedroom. I thought perhaps it was the light above the stove. The light above my stove never went off. But then, I didn't like sleeping in complete darkness, so I didn't mind.

Moonlight slanted through the windows, just enough to gild his face in a silvery glow. I wanted to trace my fingertips along his jawline and press a kiss on the side of his neck. I forced myself to hold still, but it took effort. Maybe, if I'd ever let myself fall asleep with anyone, I would've known this was a normal feeling. Maybe.

A part of me didn't *ever* want to leave. I felt so comfortable and warm. Another part of me, the opposing side, experienced this urge to leap out of bed and run bare naked across the hallway in the darkness. Since Cooper and I had the only two apartments up here, I didn't have to worry about anybody seeing me.

I seriously contemplated this option for several long moments. Yet this awakened part of me, an almost soft, animal side, had a stronger hold. I stayed right there, pressed against him. My eyes fell closed, and I slipped back into sleep.

Sometime later, I woke again to the sound of water running in the shower. I could smell coffee. I reached my arm across the sheets to find them holding just a hint of warmth. I wondered how long I had been sleeping alone, but figured it couldn't have been too long.

I heard the water turn off and sat up abruptly, the covers falling in a rumple at my waist. I intended to get up and put my clothes on when I recalled that they were in the dryer in the very bathroom where Cooper was.

Before I could make a move, he appeared in the doorway, one towel wrapped around his waist as he scrubbed his hair with another.

My mouth went dry. I had gotten a feel of *all* of Cooper last night, but it had been more of a jumble of intense sensations, not a clear sense. I hadn't taken a long look. I did now. His body was a fucking work of art. His build was lean and rangy with broad shoulders, arms strong and long, and his chest muscled with defined planes. So help me God, the man had abs.

The dusting of dark hair on his chest narrowed to a trail that arrowed straight down behind his towel. He lowered his arm, his curls damp and his dark eyes studying me before his lips kicked up at the corner. My belly swooped, and my hormones let out a raucous cheer.

"Mornin'."

The single word with a hint of a Southern drawl and butterflies tickled my belly with sparks leaping through me.

I felt his eyes drop down, and my nipples tightened. I knew I was blushing all over. When his eyes lifted again, I could feel the heat banked in his gaze from across the room.

"Good morning," I managed to say.

"There's coffee." He angled his head to the side in the direction that would be across the hall toward my apartment. "I can pop over and grab some clothes for you if you tell me where and what to get."

"Uh," I began in a raspy squeak. "You can just get my clothes out of the dryer."

"I already got your clothes out of the dryer," he offered. "They're in the bathroom on the counter."

"Oh. Okay."

Somehow, I dredged up some composure even though I was bare naked and my nipples were so very happy to see Cooper with only a towel wrapped around his waist. I got up and went to take a shower.

When I came out a few minutes later, fully dressed, he was also fully dressed. I was simultaneously disappointed and relieved.

He handed me a cup of coffee before gesturing to a container of cream on the counter. "Not sure how you like it." He took a swallow from his own mug.

I needed my coffee plain and strong this morning. I took several swallows, bracing myself to face him and somehow manage a conversation before I escaped across the hallway.

When he finally turned to look at me, I said, "Um..."

Great. I was off to a brilliant start.

After a moment, he prompted, "Yes?"

Chapter Twenty-One

COOPER

Farrah blinked and took a gulp of coffee. After she lowered her mug, she gripped it tightly. "We don't have to make last night a thing."

I studied her for a beat before nodding in agreement. "We don't."

I'd spent the approximately twenty-five minutes since I had woken with her naked body draped against mine, telling myself this was no different from any casual night. No different at all.

I studiously ignored the corner of my mind that pointed out that I'd never experienced the intensity I felt with Farrah. Whenever that voice chimed in, my rational, cynical mind would counter it. *You don't even know what that means. It's just sex. Really fucking good sex.*

"We're friends," I added. "And if we sometimes enjoy some benefits, that's okay."

"It's convenient," she chimed in, nodding vigorously.

I was both relieved and disappointed at how quickly she agreed with me. Just then, Humpty twined around her ankles, purring up a storm.

After leaning down to pet him, she straightened. "All your windows are closed, right?"

"I already double-checked. Don't worry."

Farrah collected her keys and purse minutes later, and I walked her to the door. She paused, looking up at me. The draw to kiss her was so strong, it ran roughshod over any restraint I had. The next thing I knew, I nudged her chin up with my knuckles and leaned down to give her a lingering kiss.

It was just a kiss, just a brush of my lips over hers, just a moment more to dally. I savored the brief taste of her. When I lifted my head and stared into her eyes for several beats of my heart, she looked startled. She blinked, and I could've sworn she almost shook her head.

I forced myself to step back, and then she was gone, calling over her shoulder, "See you later!"

I didn't even notice closing the door, but I leaned against it, needing the support. My head fell back, and I took a deep breath. "What the fuck am I doing?"

"Dude, you're already married," Wes said as he chuckled.

Jonah rolled his eyes. "I didn't want to wait."

"Not to be nosy—" I began.

Just as Beck interjected, "But you are being nosy."

I slid my gaze to his. "I learned from the master... You," I deadpanned. Beck burst out laughing while Jonah chuckled. "Back to my question. Why did you get married so fast?"

Jonah had recently married Alice, after starting to date her just this past summer.

He angled his head to the side, his gaze sobering.

"Well, I love her, so that part's easy. But have you met my grandmother?"

"I think so. Maybe at Firehouse Café?"

"Probably. She's friends with Janet. She's also nosy as hell. Before you know it, she'll be setting you up with someone, so watch out. I love her to pieces, and she has cancer."

"Oh fuck, man. I'm sorry. Cancer sucks."

"No shit. She's already had chemo more than once, so she's passing on it this time. She says she doesn't want to feel like shit anymore. She really wanted Alice and me to be together."

Beck cut in again, "And, conveniently, it worked out."

Jonah flashed him a wry smile. "It did. We wanted to get married while my grandmother's still around."

"That means something. And if you know, you know."

We were at Wildlands, a local favorite hangout. It was a lodge on the waters of a lake in town that catered to tourists during the summer and stayed busy throughout the year with the restaurant and bar. It had an outdoorsy vibe with wide plank hardwood flooring and exposed wooden beams crisscrossing the ceiling. With Willow Brook on the edge of the wilderness in Alaska, this was a draw for tourists in the summer months.

We'd commandeered a large round table in the corner. In the few months I had been here, a mix of us from the firefighter crews got together here, usually once a week. So far tonight, it was Beck, Chase, Wes, Jonah, Ward, and me.

Just then, Levi Phillips came striding up to the table, hooking his hand around the only empty chair left and sitting down. "Hey, guys." He glanced around. "Did you already order food? I'm fucking starving."

As if on cue, our server arrived just then. He served beers to those of us who had already ordered, took Levi's drink order, and everyone's food orders.

"Your timing was perfect," Beck said as the server hurried off.

"Is everyone on your crew back in town now?" Ward asked.

Levi nodded. "Those of us who got stuck because of engine problems with the helicopter just returned this afternoon."

Beck held his beer aloft. "Here's hoping we're almost done with fires for the season."

"How far into autumn does fire season usually last?" I asked.

Ward wiggled his hand back and forth as he took a swallow of his beer. Lowering it, he replied, "It varies. Between the three crews, we'll probably rotate out at least once or twice more. These days, though, the season seems to be stretching longer. Summers are drier and warmer. Once the snow stays farther north, we should be good to go. It's not that fires don't start at all in the winter, but they don't spread much because the snow helps contain them."

"What do we handle in the winter?" I asked.

Beck chimed in, "We cover for the town crew here when they need us and do training stuff. If needed, we head to the Lower 48 to help with fires. That's not too often, but maybe once or twice. It's nice for it to be quieter, though. If you like to ski or do any back-country stuff for the winter, you'll enjoy winter here."

A while later, after we had finished eating, Alice, Jonah's new wife, appeared. She smiled around the table. "Hey, guys." She rested her hand on Jonah's shoulder. "Going to be ready to go soon?"

From behind her, Tiffany and Farrah approached. The moment I saw Farrah weaving through the tables, awareness sizzled down my spine and my body tightened. I hadn't seen her for three days. Three days that stretched too long in my mind. She'd danced through my thoughts every fucking spare moment. Falling asleep was an exercise in trying to shut off the replay of our night together.

Her eyes met mine as she got closer to the table, and I saw awareness flickering there. Her steps faltered for a beat. Tiffany stopped beside Wes and said something. Whether or not anyone noticed the fact that Farrah and I stared at each other for what had to be a full minute, I didn't know. I was fully caught up at that moment with the heat and electricity sparking between us.

Chapter Twenty-Two

FARRAH

I had to drag my eyes away from Cooper's, trying to ignore the heat rampaging through me. My pulse raced so fast that my breath was short. People all around us were laughing, talking, eating, and drinking, basically carrying on like normal people did in social situations.

Meanwhile, I was awash in desire, feeling restless and unsettled. I had actively avoided Cooper since our night together. That in itself was unnerving for me. I literally craved seeing him. I had *missed* him.

I'd never missed a man before. I didn't crave anyone. This wasn't something that happened to me. I kept trying to convince myself it was just that we seemed to have this lightning in a bottle kind of chemistry. The kind that didn't come along very often and was startling in its intensity.

I took an unsteady breath and swallowed as I forced myself to look around the table. I shifted on my feet, my eyes drawn to Cooper again. When I met his gaze this time, I thought I saw understanding mingling with a flare of protectiveness. It actually made me feel better. Holy hell. What was happening to me?

I managed to take another shaky breath. When Alice said something to me, I turned to her. "What?"

———

"Hey!" a voice said behind me as I walked across the parking area behind Wildlands.

Before I even turned around, I knew it was Cooper, and not just because I recognized his voice. I could literally feel him approaching me from behind. My boots scuffed on the gravel as I turned and waited. He stopped a few feet away, and I could feel the voltage reverberating between us.

"Hey," I said, stuffing my hands in my jacket pockets.

"Are you walking home?" he asked.

"Uh-huh."

"Mind if I walk with you?"

"Of course not."

Without another word, I turned, and Cooper fell into step beside me.

It was maybe a ten-minute walk from Wildlands to the building beside Firehouse Café where our apartments were. We didn't even talk. I was both comforted and electrified by his presence. I wanted him with such fierceness, I couldn't talk myself out of it.

He held the door for me when we got to the building, making sure it was locked behind us before we walked up the stairs together. Our footsteps echoed on the hardwood floor after we crested the top of the stairs and turned down our shared hallway. I stopped before we reached our doors, which were directly across from each other. I looked up at him, instantly caught in the beam of his gaze.

I opened my mouth to say something, but he took a step closer and lifted his hand, brushing a lock of hair off my cheek. His fingertips trailed along the side of my neck, sending sparks leaping over my skin.

I let out a frayed breath, scrambling to gather some kind of composure. The second I lifted my eyes to his, the heat pooling low in my belly turned molten.

He studied me, and I felt as if his eyes alone were reaching through the layers wrapped around my heart. On the one hand, what I felt was pure need and raw passion. Yet spun within those silken fiery threads was an intense intimacy, tugging loose emotions that I'd kept wound tightly behind layers and layers of protection.

His hand slid to cup the side of my neck, his thumb moving in an idle pass over my thrumming pulse. All of my awareness narrowed to that tiny patch of skin with licks of fire emanating from his touch.

And then, his mouth was on mine, claiming it with a bold, masterful kiss. I could've kissed Cooper for days. His kisses alone were enough to push me to my very edge. They were all-consuming, thorough, and intense. His kisses embodied attention to detail. I sighed into his mouth, my knees liquid. I was melting all over, in thrall to him as he slid an arm around my waist, holding me firmly against his strong body.

I had no idea how much time had elapsed when we finally broke apart. It took an effort to lift my eyes. "Your place or mine?" he asked.

"It doesn't matter," I rasped.

"Mine then."

I didn't even question why until we stumbled through his door and Humpty meowed. I wanted to grasp Cooper and pull him back to me when he stepped away.

"I have to fill his food bowl." He shrugged unapologetically as he crossed to a small table by the end of the kitchen counter. A moment later, Humpty was happily eating, and Cooper was walking back to me.

I was so awash with need, my thoughts hazed with it, my attention centered solely on Cooper, that I barely registered that I had walked over to the kitchen counter. He stopped in front of me, his gaze sweeping up and down. He opened his mouth to say something just as I reached for him, fisting my hand around the fabric of his shirt.

"Come here."

He obeyed my raspy command, and a moment later, we were kissing and yanking at each other's clothes. We were rushed and messy and fumbled, and I didn't care. All I knew was the fierce rush of desire driving us forward.

When I was naked, he lifted me, spinning me to slide my hips onto the counter before he filled me. It started there and ended in his bed. In his bedroom, I was on my knees, and I felt the press of his fingertips on my hips as he filled me from behind and teased me to a climax with his fingers when he reached around.

A while later, we were resting in his bed, and I felt his fingertip trace along the scar on the side of my back, just above my hipbone. I tensed slightly, but ignored the worry that started to build.

"What happened?" he asked quietly.

"I fell and cut myself on a broken vase." My voice was steady, and I was telling the truth. I just left out the part about why I fell and why the vase was broken.

Blessedly, he left the topic alone, simply smoothing his palm over the scar as if he could make it all better.

We fell asleep later. That one corner of my mind

that was usually so noisy, prodding and poking at me, reminding me of all the reasons I couldn't trust any man, was uncharacteristically quiet. I came awake in the darkness to the sound of a cat purring. I felt my lips curve into a smile. Humpty had nestled himself between our feet.

The weirdest part was I fell right back to sleep. I couldn't remember a time in my life when I fell back asleep after I woke up during the night.

With Cooper, I felt safe.

I felt like I belonged here. With him.

And *that* was terrifying.

Chapter Twenty-Three

COOPER

The days and nights rolled on by. Farrah and I fell into a rhythm. We spent *almost* every night together. Or that was what I told myself. *Almost* was where I fudged the truth. It was every freaking night. We just didn't talk about it. Maybe that made it seem accidental.

We shifted between our places and developed a habit of closing the door at the top of the hallway so Humpty could move between our apartments at his leisure. Every time I wondered if this was getting out of hand, I shoved that question out of the way, kicking it into oblivion in my brain. We were on the same page. She didn't want more, and neither did I.

The arrangement was perfect—friends with smoking-*hot* benefits.

It was getting so comfortable that I didn't even consider it a problem until my mom came for her planned visit.

I was bringing my mother to show her my apartment, and Rowan's mother was with us. "This is a cute little building!" my mother exclaimed as we walked up the stairs.

When we turned at the top, and my hand closed over the knob of the door into the upper hallway, I realized my mother would discover I left my door open for Humpty. As did Farrah. Fuck.

Humpty sat on the windowsill at the end of the hallway in his new favorite place. The sunny spot offered a view into the trees out behind the building. He enjoyed watching the birds flit around, or so I imagined.

Humpty turned and eyed us. "Is that your cat?" my mother asked.

I immediately improvised. "That's him. He's figured out how to open the door." I shrugged.

Walking ahead, I stopped in front of Farrah's door. Fortunately, it was only open a sliver. I gestured toward my door. My mother ignored me and walked past me to greet Humpty.

Rowan's mother glanced to the other side of the hallway. I knew she noticed that Farrah's door was cracked open. I said nothing. They walked into my place a moment later, and I quickly closed Farrah's door behind me.

You are getting way too comfortable with Farrah, my skeptical mind pointed out.

I ignored it. After my very brief apartment tour, I made sure Humpty was firmly put in my apartment. I took them over to Firehouse Café. Rowan met us there, and Janet even sat down with us for a few minutes.

She smiled at my mother. "We love having Cooper here in town. I'm sure you miss him, though."

My mother smiled up at me. "Of course I do, but I'm glad he likes it here. For now," she added.

After getting a list of things to do from Janet, Rowan's mother went to the bathroom. Rowan stepped away from the table to take a phone call. My mother looked over at me. "I hope you're not planning to stay here long term. This is just temporary, right?"

"Mom, I don't know my plans. You've been traveling a lot, and the house is for sale," I pointed out.

My mother took a swallow of her tea, twisting her lips to the side. "Be that as it may, I still think you need closure with Cindy."

I resisted the urge to grit my teeth and swear. I understood that, for my mother, my breakup with Cindy had shattered her dream. The dream where I settled down in town with my high school sweetheart and the daughter of one of her closest friends. We would all be one big happy family. That wasn't going to happen.

Not for the first time, I wished my father were still here. Maybe he would know how to help my mother accept this reality. He would've had a much stronger reaction to what Cindy did. While my mother had initially experienced her own sense of betrayal at the situation, I suppose in her grief around my father, she just wanted something to stay the same. It was too much of a change for her.

"Mom, the closure has happened. For me. Maybe not for Cindy, and maybe not for her mom. But it has for me. It is what it is. I don't know what's going to happen in the future. Right now, I have no plans to move back to Stolen Hearts Valley."

My mother's fingers tightened around the handle of her mug. "I just wish..."

When her words trailed off, I cocked my head to the side, eyeing her warmly. "I know you wish things were different. They're not. Things started with Cindy and Dan before Dad died. I guess they just really heated up after that. I would've found out one way or another. Stolen Hearts Valley is too small for a secret like that to stay hidden forever. I'm just grateful I found out before Cindy and I got married."

My mother blinked, her mouth curling down at one side. My heart felt cold for a beat when I saw the grief passing through her eyes. She and my father had had the kind of love many people envied. Life hadn't been perfect for them, just as it never was for anyone, but they really had always been there for each other. Maybe, *big* maybe, I could've gotten over Cindy cheating on me, but not with one of my friends and not with the excuse that I hadn't been emotionally available enough after my dad died. Because when life got bumpy was when you were supposed to be there for each other. That was what I believed.

My mother straightened in her chair, lifting her chin. "I'm selling the house. I don't know what I'm planning to do. But with you gone and your dad gone—"

I felt compelled to clarify. "Mom, I'm not *gone* the way Dad is."

She rolled her eyes instead of bursting into tears, which was a relief. "I know."

My heart stung fiercely. I hadn't meant to be so blunt. "I'm sorry."

My mother tipped her head to the side, eyeing me thoughtfully with a sheen of tears in her eyes as she held my gaze. "It's okay. I know you didn't mean that to be hurtful. And you're right. You're alive and well and living the life you want. I suppose I've hung on to this idea because I thought maybe you and Cindy were somehow going to—" She paused, her eyes closing and her shoulders rising with a deep breath. "Going to be what your father and I were," she added when she opened her eyes again. "But you're not." She paused again to take a swallow of her tea. "I hope maybe you can find someone."

Farrah sashayed into my thoughts, and I swatted her away. I didn't need to be thinking about her like that. I shrugged. "Maybe. You and Dad had something not everyone gets."

"I know," my mother said softly. "I guess I just hope Cindy's actions didn't make you too cynical."

I heard the door to the café open, the sound of the little bell heralding another round of customers. I shouldn't have known Farrah had entered, but I did. I knew without even looking that when I glanced over, she would be there. And she was. She walked in with Tiffany, saying something to her before lifting her gaze to look around the café. Her eyes snapped into the line of my gaze, sending a jolt of electricity sizzling across the room between us.

"Who is that?" My mother's tone was a little too curious.

I glanced back toward her, marshaling my composure. In the most bland, casual tone I could muster, I replied, "Just my neighbor."

"Oh really?"

Blessedly, Janet happened to be making the rounds and collecting dishes from tables. She paused beside us. "How was your tea?" she asked my mother.

"Delicious." My mother set her mug on the table. "Tell me, Janet." She leaned forward, resting her elbows on the table. "How is Cooper doing here in Alaska?"

Janet glanced back and forth between us, her lips teasing with a smile. "I know we're happy he's here. Like I mentioned, I can imagine it's hard to have him so far from home."

Rowan's mother returned to the table. Janet got

drawn away by a customer nearby. Tiffany approached the table. Farrah wasn't with her, and I knew I shouldn't feel disappointed. But I was anyway.

"Hey, Tiffany," I said, dipping my head. I gestured to my mother. "This is my mother, Donna. And this is—"

Before I could add more, Rowan's mother chimed in. "Rowan's mother, Linda. We're here together for a visit."

Tiffany's smile widened. "Well, it's very nice to meet you both. I'm Tiffany. I work at the vet clinic and keep up with all the firefighter gossip because I'm dating one."

Rowan's mother laughed softly. "There are certainly plenty in town from what I can tell."

While I was busy telling myself not to worry about whether Farrah was still with Tiffany, that maybe she had left, she appeared beside our table. Tiffany slipped her hand through Farrah's elbow. "And this is our vet tech. This is Cooper's mom, Donna, and Rowan's mom, Linda."

My mother practically beamed at Farrah. "Hi. So nice to meet you! I love your name, by the way."

Farrah smiled politely while Tiffany chuckled. "She was named after Farrah Fawcett. Can you believe it?"

My mother's brows hitched up, and she cast me a sly look. "I used to love *Charlie's Angels*. As a result, I'm pretty sure Cooper had a crush on Farrah Fawcett in high school."

I was profoundly relieved I was not prone to blushing. I looked at my mother. "Seriously, Mom?" I deadpanned.

She shrugged, completely unabashed. "Well, it's a funny story."

Farrah piped up, "My mother loved the show, so

she named me after her. It is what it is, I suppose." When Farrah's eyes met mine, her cheeks had the slightest tinge of pink.

I had to force myself to look away. We got through a few minutes of polite conversation before Tiffany and Farrah left. As soon as they were through the door to the café and outside, my mother looked over at me. "You could have a crush on her. Maybe she needs a boyfriend. Farrah is lovely." She waggled her eyebrows.

"Mom," I ground out. "Don't start with the matchmaking."

Chapter Twenty-Four

FARRAH

You don't miss Cooper. It's just a friends-with-benefits arrangement. Nothing more.

I looked around my apartment, resisting the urge to sigh. I missed Cooper. A lot. This was the second night his mother was visiting. I told myself not to text him and not to walk across the hallway and knock on his door.

I also missed Humpty. I was going to have to get my own cat. This whole "situationship" with Cooper had gotten far too comfortable.

Glancing at the clock, I thought I should order some takeout. Just as I was about to call for pizza, I heard footsteps turning into the hallway from the stairs. I listened way too carefully. I wanted to think they were stopping outside my door, but Cooper's door was directly across the hallway from mine, so that didn't mean much.

My pulse lunged when there was a light knock on my door. I was shameless. I practically ran across the room to answer. When I swung the door open, Cooper stood there. He had one hand curled around the edge of the doorframe and the other with his thumb hooked in his pocket. I simply stood there for a long moment, soaking him in. His lips were curled at one corner and his eyes dark as his gaze locked on mine.

"Hey there, Farrah." His subtle Southern drawl slid over me, sending my belly into a spinning flip.

"Hey, Cooper."

"Can I come in?" he asked.

I took a shallow breath, stepping back as I opened the door wider. "Of course."

"How's Humpty?" I asked as he walked inside.

"He misses you. Can I let him come over?"

"Of course." I was smiling, my cheeks almost aching from it.

"Just a sec." He crossed the hall and opened his door.

Humpty dashed across the hallway into my apartment, twining around my ankles and then Cooper's. I lifted him, scratching under his chin while he purred madly. When I lowered him to the floor, he ran over to check the food and water bowl that I had here just for him.

"Should we close the doors?" I asked as I added some fresh water to his bowl.

"Probably. My mom is out with her friend tonight, but I wouldn't put it past her to stop by unexpectedly."

He closed his door and returned to my apartment, also closing the door. Humpty had made himself comfortable on the windowsill looking out over Main Street.

I was unaccountably nervous. I stood by the kitchen counter, tracing my fingertips along the curved edge. Cooper walked over, stopping in front of me.

"It was nice to meet your mom," I offered.

He nodded. "She'll be here another few days. She's with Rowan Coles's mom. He's also from Stolen Hearts Valley."

"It's nice they could travel together."

He smiled slowly. Butterflies spun inside my belly, sending tingles throughout my body.

"I love seeing my mom, but this way, she has company, and it makes it a little easier for me to host."

We studied each other. My heartbeat picked up its pace, stumbling faster and faster. Cooper stepped closer to me, his hand falling to the counter to curl over mine. His next words startled me.

"I've missed you."

My heart tumbled in my chest. "I've missed you too." Those words rushed out in a whisper.

"You seem nervous." He lifted my hand, turning it over as he dipped his head and pressed a kiss in the center of my palm. That kiss felt like a warm stone, sending ripples of heat in its wake.

I took a breath, willing my nerves to settle. There was all that chemistry that we shared lighting up like a firecracker inside. But, at this moment, it wasn't just chemistry. It was that sense of intimacy that kept building between us, spinning like gossamer threads and weaving tighter and tighter together.

"I don't think we're supposed to miss each other," I said softly, trying to ignore the tangle of emotion and need inside.

Cooper lowered my hand, still holding it in his as he stepped closer and brushed my hair away from my face. "Maybe not, but I still missed you."

My heart tripped and stumbled in my chest. I felt raw and unguarded. I felt the brush of his fingers as he tucked my hair behind my ear, and goose bumps prickled over my skin.

When he bent low and brushed his lips over mine, liquid heat spun through my veins, pooling low in my belly. I let out a little whimper as I leaned closer. For the first time in days, I felt that sense of coming home, a feeling I hadn't put words to and had purposely shied away from.

But when Cooper's arms slid around my waist and he held me against him with his firm, strong hold, I felt protected, safe, exactly where I wanted and needed to be.

One kiss blurred into the next. He undressed me slowly, and I felt cherished in a way I had never felt. We were often rushed, despite more than enough nights together to slow down. Nothing ever felt choreographed with us. Tonight, though, our time together was a slow, deeply sensual encounter.

He lifted me into his arms after tossing my shirt to the floor and teasing my nipples to the point of pain.

"I don't think I can stand," he said a few moments later as he stretched me out on the bed before him.

His palm slid in a sure caress over my belly, sparks leaping in the wake of his touch. I trembled underneath him when he trailed kisses between my breasts and down my belly. I felt molten inside, nearly quivering with anticipation. I cried out when he brought his mouth to my sex and licked deeply into me. I heard myself, a part of me I didn't even recognize, as I panted his name. I *needed* him inside me when I came.

I tugged at his shoulders. "Cooper, please, I need you. Now."

He didn't even tease, rising to hover above me. Somewhere along the way, he'd already rolled a condom on.

"You have me," he said just as he notched himself at my entrance, his eyes holding mine.

In a slow, deliberate motion, he sank into me. My heart raced as I sighed at the delicious stretch of him filling me. I savored the slick friction of our joining when he seated himself deeply before drawing back and surging to fill me again.

When his weight came over me, it felt just right. I was caught between feeling spun out of control inside and protected by him, by his presence.

My orgasm built quickly. When he reached between us to tease over my clit, creating just enough pressure to push me over the edge, the pleasure came in deep surges, rocking me to my core. I cried out, feeling him follow me over the edge as the heat of his release filled me when he plunged into me one final time, shuddering deeply.

Whenever he was on top of me like this, he moved to roll over. I felt protected, savored, and cared for. I rested against him, almost shocked at the depth of intimacy I felt between us.

When I pulled myself together and slowly rose on an elbow to look at him, his eyes met mine. My heart kicked hard against my ribs. I wanted this. I wanted him. I wanted this feeling between us. And I was *never* supposed to want that from anyone.

Chapter Twenty-Five

COOPER

The following morning, I woke early. Nothing about that was unusual. I felt utterly relaxed and sated. Farrah was curled against me. She usually slept like this, pressed against my side with her head tucked into the curve of my shoulder with one knee hooked over my thigh and her foot tucked between my calves. Her arm was curled over me with her palm resting on the edge of my rib cage. I had an arm wrapped around her with my hand splayed at the dip of her waist, my fingers just over the sweet curve of her bottom. I felt my lips curving into a smile in the darkness. Humpty purred where he slept at our feet, something else that had become a habit so swiftly I didn't know what to make of it. I tried to remind myself that Farrah and I were on the same page. This wasn't anything big.

Ha! My cynical mind scoffed.

I wasn't supposed to miss Farrah, yet I had. A mere two nights had passed where I hadn't seen her. Both nights, I'd had dinner with my mother. That had been my reason for not seeing Farrah. That and trying to remind myself we were just friends with *really* good benefits.

Who the fuck are you kidding? You didn't even feel this way about Cindy.

I had loved Cindy. I really had. Maybe it was because we'd been younger when it all started, but we certainly hadn't had the molten-hot chemistry I felt with Farrah. Holy hell, the heat of it was enough to burn us to the ground. I kept thinking it would start to cool. Instead, the opposite was happening. Every encounter stoked the flames higher and higher.

Farrah shifted in her sleep, making a soft sound I loved, something between a breath and a sigh. I fell back asleep. Because, even if my mind was spinning its wheels, I felt good when I was with her.

———

It was the last day of my mother's visit here, and we were at Firehouse Café. I was laughing at something Rowan's mother said when Rowan nudged me with his elbow. I glanced his way. Our mothers were distracted and looking at a moose walking down the side street visible from the café.

He discreetly nodded his head toward the doorway, and I looked over.

"Fuck," I muttered before I could catch myself.

Cindy had just walked in. She looked around the café, and her eyes met mine. I wasn't even angry she was here. I was just resigned at what was about to play out.

She smiled brightly, walking over quickly. "Hi!" she exclaimed.

My mother swung to look her way. "Oh!" My

mother looked legitimately surprised, while Rowan's mother looked annoyed.

"Hi, Cindy," I said as I stood from the table. "You can have my seat."

She moved to hug me, but she must've read my look because she stepped back.

"I thought with your mom and Rowan's mom visiting, it was a perfect time for me to come for a surprise visit. We're a little contingent from Stolen Hearts Valley." Cindy's smile was a little forced.

I heard Rowan's reply under his breath. "Not sure how that makes a lick of sense."

God only knows how, but we shifted into small talk, most of the conversation carried by my mother and Linda.

As if this shit show couldn't get worse, Farrah walked in with Tiffany and Wes.

It wasn't like I had to greet everyone I knew in Firehouse Café, but it would be near impossible to ignore them. Moments later, the three of them were beside the table, and Cindy was introducing herself as my "ex-fiancée, I guess" as she kept trying to catch my eye.

Farrah's eyes lifted to mine, and I could see the questions swirling there. All I wanted was for Cindy to get the fuck out of here and to steal a few minutes alone with Farrah to explain this mess.

The next few hours were a special version of hell. My mother, of course, didn't feel right just leaving Cindy alone, so she wanted her to come with us. She pulled me aside. "I had no idea Cindy was planning this. You know I can't leave Brenda's daughter alone here."

"Mom, Cindy is *not* staying with me, and y'all are due at the airport soon."

I drove them all back to the airport after telling Cindy she couldn't stay with me. Cindy wanted to "talk" with me, so I found a spot in the parking garage after my mother and Rowan's mother headed for the gate.

"Okay, what's up?" I asked once I was parked. "There's nothing left for us to talk about, but you said you wanted to talk."

Cindy blurted out, "My flight doesn't leave for a week."

I looked over at her for a long moment. "Cindy, you're not staying with me, and I'm not hosting you for a visit around town. You can get a hotel here in Anchorage. You can do whatever the fuck you want. I don't know what you think you're doing, but you and I are not getting back together. I'm not mad at you anymore. I wish you and Dan the best."

Cindy burst into tears. My jaw tightened, and I took several slow breaths while I waited. After a moment, Cindy turned away to look out the window. She took a sniffling breath and glanced back toward me. She swiped at the tears rolling down her cheeks and fumbled for a tissue in her purse before blowing her nose.

At one time, the sight of Cindy crying would've elicited the urge to comfort her, to make it all better. I didn't feel any of that right now. I meant what I said. I wasn't mad at her anymore, but whatever we once had was gone for me. I cared for her in a detached way.

After a moment, she whispered my name, twisting the tissue in her hands. "I thought we could try again."

I bit the insides of my cheeks to keep from sighing. "Cindy, I'm really not mad at you, but we can't try again. I don't want to try again, and I never will."

"I want to try!" she burst out, her eyes narrowing.

I studied her, taking in the face I knew so well. She had honey-blond hair on the dark side. Her eyes were big and brown. She had a little spray of freckles on her cheeks that I used to love. Now when I looked at her, I experienced an objective appreciation of her beauty and nothing more.

I didn't want to rehash this discussion. At all. But here we were.

"I don't want to try again, Cindy. I'm assuming things aren't working out very well with you and Dan if you flew all the way here for this," I pointed out, striving for a gentle tone.

She sniffled and shrugged. "We broke up."

At one time, learning this detail would've felt satisfying. The anger I initially experienced when I learned about their shared betrayal had been white hot. It had faded, and now there was just a twinge, a reminder of why trust wasn't worth it.

"Well, I'm sorry to hear that," I finally said.

"Is what I did unforgivable?" she pressed, her tone bordering on annoyance.

"I *have* forgiven you, but I don't think you understand that forgiveness doesn't mean I want to try again. Forgiveness also doesn't mean I'm stupid. I said it before, but I guess you need to hear it again. I understand that I might not have been the most emotionally available guy after my dad died. Instead of trying to be there for me and understanding what I was going through, you cheated on me with my friend. I'm sorry to hear you and Dan didn't work out. I understand you want to try again with us, but I'm just not there, and I won't ever be. I hope for your sake that you've learned from this. I'm not the person for you to try to make it right with. You're going to have to find your own way through this."

She chewed on the inside of her cheek and kept twisting the tissue between her fingers to the point it was fraying. "Cooper, I wasn't thinking. I guess you got what you wanted. Dan and I didn't work out, and now I'm dragging around the reputation that I screwed around on my fiancé with his friend after his dad died. You wouldn't believe the way people look at me in town."

"I'm sorry to hear that, Cindy. We're not here today because of what I wanted. What I wanted was for us to work out. I don't anymore. Forgiveness doesn't mean everything goes back to the way it was. You're going to have to figure this out yourself. I think you think us being back together will make it all better, but it won't. This would always be between us because it isn't just that you cheated on me. It's that you weren't there for me when I needed you. I would always wonder if you couldn't handle being there for me when things were hard. You *will* find someone else, and you can take the lessons from this to that relationship."

She blinked, and a single tear rolled down her cheek. "I'm sorry," she whispered.

For the very first time, I sensed her apology was heartfelt. "I'm sorry too. Now, I'd suggest you go into the airport, change your flight, and fly home. Maybe you and Dan will figure things out, or maybe you'll meet someone new. I wish you the best."

Cindy could be stubborn, a trait of hers I was very familiar with, but she appeared to recognize this was final. Her cheating on me had screwed up more for her than our relationship. Before that, she had a good reputation in our small town. I had enough sense to know that what others thought of you could be a bunch of bullshit. Everybody made mistakes, many of them not so public. But now, she had to live with these mistakes and learn to ignore how others viewed her or prove them wrong.

I drove around to the departure zone, and she climbed out of my truck. I did not give her a hug when I got her bags out for her. She peered up at me, her gaze a mix of hopeful and uncertain. "Have a safe trip," I offered.

I waited there on the curb beside my truck in the drop-off area as she walked through the doors into the airport, glancing back one more time to wave.

A few minutes later, I was driving home, my thoughts on Farrah.

Chapter Twenty-Six

FARRAH

"Who?" I asked.

Janet handed over my change, and I promptly stuffed it in the tip jar.

"Cindy, his former fiancée," Janet said, sotto voce.

"How do you know this?" I hated how curious I was. Until I'd met his ex, I'd had no idea Cooper had previously been engaged.

Janet shrugged. "I hear everything. His mother and Rowan's mother were talking about it. I guess Cindy cheated on him with a friend after Cooper's father died. Of course, that didn't work out. Apparently, she came here to win Cooper back. He wanted nothing to do with it. I don't even know what she was thinking. I suppose she thought creating a public spectacle would make something happen." Janet shook her head, tsk-tsking.

"Oh," I said, trying to keep my tone bland. I knew about the cheating, but I hadn't known they'd been engaged when it happened.

Janet cocked her head to the side. "Cooper is a good man."

"I know he is."

"I know you two have a thing going on."

I had just taken a swallow of my coffee and sputtered on it. She quickly handed me a napkin. I dabbed at the corners of my mouth.

"I don't know what you're talking about," I hedged.

Janet arched a brow. "Sure you do. Don't worry, I would never say anything to anyone about it. But, you forget, I'm your landlady. And there's a security camera in the hallway up there."

Heat flared in my cheeks. "Oh my God," I said slowly. "How much —"

"After that first crazy kiss in the hallway, I turned it off. You can rest assured. I only have it for safety and security. Not to be nosy."

"Oh my God," I repeated under my breath.

She chuckled. "I think you and Cooper make a cute couple."

I shrugged. "It's not like that."

Janet narrowed her eyes. "Are you trying to pretend this is one of those friends-with-benefits arrangements?"

I nodded vigorously. "Yes! He told me he's not interested in commitment, and neither am I. Clearly, he has his reasons. So do I." My words sounded more confident than I felt inside.

She studied me quietly. The understanding in her gaze made my heart ache a little.

"You know, your mom has talked to me. She wishes she could change how things went in your childhood."

My eyes stung with tears, and my throat felt tight. I managed to shrug even though my attempt at nonchalance was total bullshit. "Nobody can change the past. I'm assuming she might've told you my stepdad was an abusive asshole. I know now that it wasn't safe for her to leave, but I also know love is never worth it."

Janet didn't reply. She rounded the counter, surprising me when she pulled me into a warm, comforting embrace. When she stepped back, she looked deep into my eyes, and I felt like she was peering into my soul. "Love *is* worth it."

———

I finished chewing the last bite of a slice of pizza.

"This place is so good," my mother chimed in.

We were having pizza at a local favorite place. We often ordered takeout for lunch at the vet clinic from here.

After taking a swallow of water, I replied, "It really is."

I thought we were going to do our usual for this lunch date, a sort of comfortable conversation about the weather, my job, and the various things my mother was doing to settle into Willow Brook.

"You know how I mentioned your grandparents?"

I nodded. "Yeah?" A sense of uneasiness and trepidation slid through me.

It wasn't that I had forgotten my mother had mentioned my grandparents, but I had mastered, absolutely *mastered*, the art of compartmentalization. A part of that included never dwelling on details. It was a way to protect myself, to never expect too much from life.

"I've talked to them a few times, and they do want to visit. What do you think?"

She looked so hopeful, almost childlike, that it cracked my already achy, tired heart. She'd never been able to consider having friends or family visit when my stepfather was alive. It almost felt as if she were asking my permission, which saddened me further. She was so deeply ingrained in never making waves that I knew if I shared any hesitation, she wouldn't do it. Not that I would, but it was heartbreaking to know she would if I did.

"Not that you need my permission, but I think it's a great idea. As I said before, I'll help pay for the tickets. If you'd prefer to go see them, I'll help with that too."

My mother was quiet for a few beats, fiddling with her fork. "I think it would be better if I went there, probably."

Her brow was furrowed, and worry flickered in her gaze. She had been chronically worried for my entire life, so that was nothing new. But I felt pressed to ask, "What are you worried about?"

Her shoulders rose and fell when she took a deep breath. "I just don't know how to make it right."

"Make what right?" I thought I knew what she meant, but I wasn't entirely sure.

"I never should've stayed with Gerald, but I didn't know how to get out."

"I know." My tone was clipped, and I didn't mean for it to be.

It was just a mess. Intellectually, I understood how hard it had been for her. I just wished she had gotten out before it got so bad. If I ever forgot how bad it was, I always had the scar on my back to remind me. There were so many things that I could never talk about with her. There were hundreds of little land-mines in my relationship with my mother. We were trying to make our way through this, carefully zigzag-ging, freezing in place, and then tiptoeing forward. Sometimes we reversed course and went backward. I wanted it to be okay for us, but I didn't know how we'd ever really get there.

I scraped for composure, for my own pain not to barge into this too much. "Mom, you can't change the past. All you can do is move forward. I know Gerald didn't want you to have contact with, well, anyone. It's not like I don't get it, either. I get it intellectually, but it's still hard emotionally."

My mother stared at me, blinking rapidly. "Farrah, I would give anything to undo my choices."

"I know." My voice was a little hoarse. My heart ached, and I was tired, so very weary.

I thought about Cooper. Even though I didn't want to admit it, I knew I was in love with him. I didn't trust the universe to make it okay. Because I remembered when my mother met Gerald and it all began. He was nice. Until he wasn't. It all started with a slap. Even though I trusted Cooper, or I thought I did, I wasn't so sure I could trust my own judgment. What if it all fell apart?

I didn't just mean him becoming controlling or violent. I didn't believe that would ever happen. I just didn't know if I could ever relax. It was almost easier to keep my distance. I took a shaky breath. "Mom, it's okay. It's really okay."

She studied me before nodding. "I think I'll fly to see my parents. I think I should go first, and we'll see how it goes."

"Okay, I'll get your ticket."

"You don't—"

"Mom, I want to help," I insisted. "I can afford it."

"If you want to go with me—"

I shook my head. "Mom, one thing at a time. You go, see how it goes, and then we can go together again, or they can come up here."

When we walked outside after dinner, we hugged. It was brief, but my heart softened a little. I wanted us to be okay. I didn't know if I was disappointed with my mother, or the universe. I just wished my feelings weren't so fraught so much of the time.

After she drove away, I took a slow breath and tipped my head back to look up at the sky. The stars were bright, and clouds drifted across the moon. An owl hooted in the trees nearby with another calling in return. No matter what happened, nature simply carried on.

My mind looped back to Janet's words. *Love is worth it.*

Was it really?

Chapter Twenty-Seven

FARRAH

I told myself I was going to talk with Cooper. I wanted to backpedal somehow. I talked myself right out of it, my cynical side pointing out, *You've already had this conversation. He doesn't want anything more, and neither do you.*

That side of me, usually so pushy, wasn't much of a match for my heart. When I saw Cooper's door cracked open when I got home and Humpty seated on the windowsill at the end of the hallway, my heart soared.

Cooper must've heard my footsteps because the door swung open farther. He stood in the doorway with one hand resting high on the doorframe and his dark eyes raking over me before catching mine in an electrifying, fiery gaze.

I told myself it was just sex when we began kissing and spun into his apartment. He bent me over the counter to sink into me from behind, sending me flying with his fingers.

When we fell asleep in my bed later and I woke with Humpty purring from where he was tucked between our feet, I told myself this was all it had to be.

The following morning when Cooper made coffee before I left for work, I decided I needed to reestablish some boundaries. I suppose for myself more than anything. Because I liked Cooper. Too much. *Waaaayyyy* too much. All of it—the crazy-hot sex, the waking up with him, how I felt protected and safe with him, the craving for something like this all the time.

When Humpty trotted out to the hallway to survey the view from the hallway window, I braced myself. "So," I began. My blunt self, the part of me that easily deflected men who wanted more than one night, kicked into gear. "We've kind of slipped into a pattern."

When Cooper glanced up, his gaze was careful as he nodded. I added, "I just thought maybe I should clarify I don't want more."

Cooper had lifted his mug to take a swallow of coffee. His hand hovered in the air before he lowered the cup to the counter. His grip tightened on the handle, just slightly. After a beat, he nodded. "Okay. Thanks for the clarification, I guess."

My cheeks were hot, and I felt uncomfortable and awkward. I took a gulp of my own coffee. "How did the visit go with your ex?"

Now, why the hell did I go and ask that?

Cooper's eyes narrowed. This time he did take a swallow of coffee, his movement controlled and smooth. "Cindy didn't stay. I had no idea she was planning to show up like that. I took her back to the airport the same day she arrived. Why does that matter?"

I shrugged. "I'm not sure why I said anything."

Cooper was quiet for a few beats before adding, "Her showing up was just a reminder of why I don't want anything more either."

I didn't think he meant to hurt me, but his comment stung. It wasn't as if I could hold it against him. I was the one who'd insisted on reiterating my own stance, clarifying the boundaries we'd established before.

I blinked quickly. "I understand. I hope you know I wouldn't ever do what she did. Screwing around on someone with their friend is really fucking shitty."

"I wasn't implying you would ever do that. Just clarifying, like you did."

We stared at each other. Even though neither of us raised our voice and everything seemed calm on the surface, my heart banged against my ribs, and I felt a little sick. I wanted to cry. I'd never explained to Cooper why I didn't do relationships. I didn't *ever* explain that to anyone. Yet I knew he had heard that comment I made to my mother. I hated that he'd heard anything. I hated my own defensiveness. I hated how that knowledge was a little bomb about to go off, an ugly truth I never wanted to discuss. I didn't have it in me to discuss it.

I took a shaky breath. "I'm glad we cleared that up."

"There was nothing to clear up," he replied.

———

Halfway through work the next day, just after wrangling a wildly dramatic husky while we drew blood, I got a text from Cooper.

Cooper: *Hey, we're going out for a fire. We'll probably* *be gone at least a week. Can you take care of Humpty for me? Sorry for the short notice.*

Me: *Of course! I'll make sure he's all set. Be safe.*

My thumbs hovered over my screen. I wanted to add, "I'll miss you."

I didn't.

After I replied to him, I couldn't help but replay our conversation from earlier. It bothered me that he was leaving now. It didn't feel right, and I knew I'd miss him.

He was a hotshot firefighter, so I expected him to be gone for stretches of time. I understood that. I was trying so hard to keep my heart out of this.

It wasn't working.

Chapter Twenty-Eight

COOPER

My head fucking pounded. I leaned back against a rock behind me, reaching for a bottle of water and taking several swallows. Glancing to the side, I caught Rowan's eyes. "Can you check in the first-aid pack there? I could use some ibuprofen."

A moment later, Rowan handed over two ibuprofen. "Are you okay?"

"Think so. Just a vicious headache." I felt like shit, in general, but I was hoping the ibuprofen would knock out my headache.

He studied me for a beat, his gaze concerned. "Well, if you need anything else, say the word." He glanced at his watch. "We're supposed to get picked up in two hours."

Being exhausted at the end of a stretch out in the wilderness fighting a wildfire was par for the course and expected. Fortunately, we had this fire fully contained. The weather was on our side with some rain on the way and the wind changing direction.

Even with the expected exhaustion, this headache

took it up a notch. I would be relieved to hop on the helicopter and fly out of here.

"Do you want anything to eat?" Rowan asked next after I chased down the two pills with another swallow of water.

The thing was, I didn't have much of an appetite. I knew I needed to eat something, though. "I'll take a granola bar."

Between that and the ibuprofen, I felt marginally better a short while later. My crew was milling around. Paisley plunked down on the ground beside me, giving me a considering look. "Dude, you look like shit, and that's saying something. Our standards are so low you could trip over them out here."

I let out a dry chuckle just as her fiancé, Russell, sat down beside her and laughed at her comment. "You okay, man?" he asked.

"I feel like shit. I think maybe I have a migraine. The ibuprofen is holding it at bay a little."

Paisley's brow furrowed. "Hmm. Let us know if you need anything else."

My thoughts shifted to Farrah. I'd been thinking about her way too much. Fortunately, I didn't have much downtime. When dealing with an active fire, we hardly had any time. We were all usually so exhausted that sleep came easily.

When the helicopter arrived, my head still throbbed, only slightly less. A few hours later when we landed in Willow Brook, I trudged into the station. I got through my shower and changed into clean clothes, but it took all my energy.

As I was walking through the back area, Maisie happened to glance over, and her gaze narrowed in concern. "Cooper, are you okay?" She hurried over to my side.

"Migraine, I think." I swallowed, willing the nausea rising in my throat to dissipate.

"Oh no. Do you need anything?"

"Just to get home and go to sleep."

For the first time since that awkward conversation with Farrah the morning before I left, I couldn't even really focus on how unsettled I still felt about that. I just needed to get home and go to bed.

I couldn't really track the details, but the next thing I knew, Beck was loading me in his truck, telling me that Maisie said he had to take me home. When he walked me up the stairs, he offered, "Dude, you look like shit. Get some rest. If you need anything, you know where to reach us."

I shuffled into my apartment. I kicked the door shut before crawling into my bed, mostly dressed except for my boots and jacket. I woke hours later, shivering and aching all over.

My thoughts were fuzzy. My mind thought I needed to worry about something, but I couldn't even grasp it.

I fell back into a feverish, achy sleep.

Chapter Twenty-Nine

FARRAH

Since I understood that hotshot firefighters didn't have what could be called a regular schedule, I didn't think much of it when I hadn't heard from Cooper in over a week. Since I was taking care of Humpty, Cooper's apartment was locked. I thought nothing of it.

Until I was at work and Wes came walking in to the vet clinic. "What are you doing here?" I asked.

Wes leaned over to kiss Tiffany and straightened. He held up a cat carrier. "Dropping off this little kitten to get spayed. She should be on the schedule under the rescue program. Why so surprised?" he asked with a grin.

"I thought your crew was out dealing with a fire?"

"Yeah, we were. We got back yesterday. Haven't you seen Cooper?"

"Uh, no." Panic rose inside. "His truck's not in the parking area behind our building, and..." I felt so flustered I couldn't even finish my sentence.

Wes whipped his phone out quickly and tapped the screen before lifting it to his ear. After a moment, he lowered it. "Weird, Cooper's not answering. Let me check with Maisie. She'll know."

Maybe things were a little off with Cooper and me after our last conversation, but it didn't make sense that he didn't check on Humpty when he returned.

A moment later, I could hear Maisie answering. "Uh-huh," Wes was saying. "Oh, that explains it. Okay, I'll let Farrah know."

"I guess he had a migraine when we landed yesterday. I knew he had a headache, but I wasn't tracking him since we have twenty-five on the crew. Maisie said he looked bad enough that she asked Beck to give him a ride home. According to her, Beck even walked him up to his apartment and made sure he went in. I'm thinking maybe you should check on him when you get home tonight. I've never had a migraine, but I've heard they can be a special kind of hell," Wes explained.

Distracted with worry, I nodded, walking back to the break room as Tiffany checked in with Wes about the cat. A few minutes later, I had sent Cooper a text and tried to call him twice.

Alice appeared in the break area. "Are you ready to do some prep for that spay surgery?"

When I looked up, my concern must've been obvious. "Whoa, are you okay?" Alice walked into the room.

I opened my mouth to say something, anything, but nothing came out.

"Hey, hey," she said in a soft and soothing tone. "Breathe."

"Cooper got home yesterday."

Alice cocked her head to the side, nodding slowly. "Uh, yeah, so did Jonah."

"But I didn't know. And something's wrong. I guess

he had a migraine. But it's not like him not to check with me when he gets back. I'm taking care of Humpty, and Cooper would want to check on him. I didn't see his truck, so I didn't think anything of it. Nobody's heard from him today, and he's not answering texts or calls."

"You should go check on him," she ordered, steering me toward the hallway.

"But —"

Alice clasped me by the shoulders, her grip firm and steadying. "I love having your help, but I can handle this. I can do the prep for this surgery in my sleep. It's a spay operation, something I've done more than any other procedure. I'll get started and take care of it on my own. Until we hired you, that's what I did. You go check on Cooper. I'm sure he's probably just sleeping it off. You can see how he's doing, and then you can relax."

"Okay, okay," I said, nodding jerkily.

I grabbed my purse and jacket. Just as I was about to walk out of the break room, she added, "After you know he's okay, maybe you could think about your feelings for him."

I spun around, my mouth falling open. "I'm just worried!"

"Of course. I'm just saying there are levels of worry. You look like you're about to have a meltdown."

Too flustered to respond, all I could do was shake my head and leave.

I couldn't drive fast enough from the vet clinic to my apartment, practically skidding to a stop in the back parking area with my tires squealing a little as I threw my car in to park and rushed up the stairs. When I got to Cooper's door, I realized I didn't actually have a key to his place. I reached for the doorknob, turning it to discover it was unlocked. I was just about to walk right in when I realized I should probably knock first. Maybe he was home.

When there was no response after three attempts at knocking, I turned the knob quietly and let myself in. I tiptoed through his apartment. All the lights were out, and Cooper's jacket was on the floor below where he normally hung it on a row of hooks on the wall. He must've dropped it. His boots were beside it, laying haphazardly.

"Cooper," I called softly.

A hush greeted me. I called his name again, a little louder this time. I slipped off my shoes and walked quietly across the living room to his bedroom door. I touched it lightly with my fingertips where it was resting ajar.

"Cooper," I repeated.

I heard a ragged and strained breath, not quite a moan. Pushing the door open, I hurried across the room to his bed. The sheets were twisted around his waist. "Farrah?" he croaked.

"Cooper, are you okay? You don't sound okay."

I could hear the congestion in his lungs with every breath. I reached to turn on the lamp on his bedside table. His hair was damp, and I brushed it away from his forehead, resting the back of my hand there for a moment. He was clearly feverish, and his skin was flushed and splotchy.

His eyes opened. They were glassy and red-rimmed. "I just got home," he rasped, his throat sounding scratchy.

"No, you didn't," I muttered fiercely. "You've been home since Beck dropped you off yesterday afternoon. And you're sick!" My sharp voice notched an octave higher with each word. I tried to batten down the worry rising swiftly inside.

He shook his head, mumbling, "No, no, no. I just got home like an hour or so ago."

I took a deep breath, trying to steady my nerves. "I came over because I didn't even know you were back from the fire. When Wes came by the clinic, I realized you were home and didn't even know it. Since I have Humpty, I thought you would've called." I smoothed his hair back from his forehead. He was still dressed.

"Cooper," I said, a little more firmly this time. His eyes dragged up to mine. "Have you had ibuprofen or anything to drink or eat?" I pressed.

He rolled his head back and forth on the pillow.

"Okay. We're getting you situated. Be right back."

With worry churning uncomfortably inside, I stood and walked out of his bedroom into his kitchen. There wasn't much of anything in his refrigerator or in his cabinets.

I knew he didn't keep much stocked in his kitchen. It wasn't that he couldn't take care of himself. He had mentioned that when he went out into the backcountry, he didn't like to worry about things going bad while he was gone, so he tended to shop week to week.

I made the abrupt decision that I was going to get him over to my place one way or another. I marched back into his bedroom. "Cooper," I said firmly.

His eyes opened slowly, his gaze still glassy and weary. "I want to get you up and in the shower. Then you're going to change and come over to my place. I have soup and crackers and plenty of ibuprofen. I even have medication for the flu, if that's what you have."

He started to shake his head, but I persisted. Driven by my intense concern, I dragged that man out of bed, despite his stubborn reluctance. After getting the shower going, I helped him strip out of his clothes. He leaned on me, but he got into the shower on his own. I waited beside it, peering around the edge of the curtain again and again. With his hands braced on the wall, he showered. I darted into his bedroom, fetching a pair of boxer briefs, sweatpants, socks, and a shirt.

I planned to come back over and strip his bed once I got him resting in my bed. I'd take care of laundering his sheets later on, which were damp from his sweat.

A short while later, I had him across the hallway in my apartment. Humpty was happy to see him. Cooper clumsily petted him after I got him propped up with extra pillows on my couch.

He looked up at me. "Thank you," he said hoarsely. "I guess I have a cold or the flu, or I don't know, something that feels like shit."

"Well, we're starting with a Covid test," I said practically.

A few years into living in a world with Covid, I usually kept one or two tests in my apartment. Alice didn't want us working if we tested positive and had a firm rule that we couldn't come in if we were sick with anything, not just Covid.

I handed him some ibuprofen and a glass of water. "I'm making chicken and dumplings right now. It won't take long. For now, I'll get you some tea. Do you think you can eat anything?"

He sighed heavily. "I'm fucking starving. Obviously, I must've been asleep since yesterday. I can't fucking believe I slept into the next day."

I ignored the anxiety spinning in my chest and focused on tasks to help. A few minutes later, I handed him some saltines with a steaming mug of lemon ginger tea. In short order, the Covid test had shown negative. We did two in a row to be safe. "It looks like the flu or a nasty cold. I'm guessing the flu based on your fever. You're not going anywhere until you feel better," I ordered.

"You don't have to—"

I narrowed my eyes. "I'm not leaving you alone in your apartment. For God's sake, no one even knew where you were." I threw my hands up, letting them fall as I studied him. "Your truck is still at the fire station. Let me check on the soup."

I strode swiftly across my apartment into the kitchen. I adjusted the heat under the soup and stirred it. After that, I carefully ladled the dumplings in to simmer. I kept checking on Cooper. He had the TV on and was sort of awake. His color was marginally better between the tea, crackers, and ibuprofen.

Humpty appeared concerned and had situated himself on the back of the couch. From there, he could still see out the windows and also keep an eye on Cooper.

"This tea is really good," Cooper commented at one point, his voice raspy and weak.

My heart ached. I kept telling myself I was just worried and would be concerned for any friend, which was true. But it was more than that, and I knew it. Somehow, seeing Cooper like this, so sick and alone when I found him, brought emotions rushing fiercely to the surface. It was stupid, and I couldn't even believe it, but I'd fallen in love with this man. All I wanted was to make sure he was okay. Only then would I be able to relax.

A short while later, the dumplings bubbled on top of the chicken soup, and I had seasoned it, sticking to the simple flavors. All he needed was nourishment.

I ladled some soup in a bowl for him, placing it on

a wooden tray by the corner of the couch where he was seated. "There. Now, eat," I ordered.

After helping him sit up carefully, I grabbed a few more pillows from the other side of the couch and tucked them behind him.

After a few bites, he looked up at me. "Oh my God, thank you."

I sat down beside him. "Next time you're sick, text me, knock on my door. Anything." I was fighting back tears.

He took another bite of his soup, closing his eyes as he swallowed. When he looked back at me, he said, "I didn't mean to scare you. I honestly just crashed in my bed as soon as I got home."

I closed my eyes and took a slow breath. Opening them, I saw he was taking another bite of soup. "Okay." That was all I could manage. My emotions crested high inside, and I felt vulnerable, my reaction overblown, at least in my own brain.

Spinning restlessly inside, I stood and returned to the kitchen area. I busied myself with cleaning up. It wasn't much later when Cooper fell sound asleep in my bed. He had dozed off on the couch before I prodded him into my bedroom. I wanted to make sure he was comfortable for the night.

I checked his forehead again. He still felt feverish, but he wasn't as hot as he'd been earlier. Humpty followed me out to the living room area again as I quietly closed the bedroom door behind me. I plunked down on the couch, and the tears I'd been holding at bay rushed up, spilling down my cheeks. I'd broken my own rules. The thing I promised myself I'd never do had happened. I'd fallen in love.

"So stupid," I whispered between sniffles.

Humpty interrupted my tears to crawl behind

where my elbows rested on my knees and butt his head against my chin. I lifted my head and straightened, stroking my palm down his back.

"I'm being dramatic, huh?" I mused to him.

Humpty blinked at me and butted my chin again.

When I looked into his eyes, I could've sworn that cat knew how I was feeling.

A few minutes later, I checked on Cooper in the bedroom again. He dragged his eyes open. "Don't leave," he whispered hoarsely.

Chapter Thirty

COOPER

My memory was blurry, but I recalled waking and feeling sore and achy all over. Then I remembered Farrah beside me, wiping a cool cloth over my forehead and making sure I took ibuprofen.

Maybe it was a day later, but my sense of time was all out of whack. I came awake again to Humpty nuzzling me under my chin. Opening my eyes slowly, I found him peering down at me curiously.

I wasn't completely well, but I felt halfway there. I sat up and glanced over at the bedside table. There was a glass of water and a bottle of ibuprofen with a note taped on top of it.

I didn't want Humpty to take your ibuprofen. I went in to work. Text me when you're up. There's chicken soup in the refrigerator already in a bowl. You just have to take the lid off and heat it in the microwave. The kettle is full of water, and a mug with a bag of ginger lemon tea is ready for you. Make it. I wouldn't recommend coffee. But if you need the caffeine, there's black tea too, and there's a mug with that in it as well. Farrah

My lips curled into a smile as I shifted up farther

and leaned against the pillows. Farrah's chicken soup and dumplings had been a lifesaver last night. Oh, I wasn't under the impression that I'd been about to die, but the nourishing soup had snapped me out of my feverish, hungry, and miserable haze.

My eyes landed on the note again.

p.s. I got your phone from your apartment. It was on the floor in your jacket pocket.

I took a breath and reached for my phone, opening the screen to type out a text to her.

Me: *I'm awake and planning to get up and have some tea. Thank you for everything.*

I climbed out of bed, feeling a little weak as I made my way out of her bedroom into the kitchen area with Humpty padding along behind me. I started the kettle. I eyed the coffee maker, but my stomach wasn't ready for it. I knew I needed caffeine, so I started with the black tea and heated some soup.

My phone vibrated where I'd set it on the counter, and I checked to see if she had replied.

Farrah: *Stay put and rest. I mean that. I stripped your bed and put your sheets and towels in the washer before I left. You apparently don't have an extra set of sheets??? I'll be home at lunch.*

I chuckled softly.

Me: *I don't have extra sheets. I know I should, but it's just me. Thank you for everything. I'll see you soon.*

I felt sort of human after I took some ibuprofen and ate some soup. I settled in on the couch and nursed a mug of tea. Farrah had even left blankets and extra pillows on the couch with another note, instructing me to get comfortable in front of the TV if I couldn't fall back asleep.

Of course, my thoughts were filled with her. I had missed her. *Soooo* fucking much.

I knew I wanted more. I wanted *all* of it with her. Between Farrah pointedly clarifying her boundaries before I left for the fire and my encounter with Cindy, my feelings for Farrah had become startlingly clear.

I recalled my mother saying more than once in the time since Cindy and I had broken up that I wasn't the kind of guy to be a bachelor forever. That I was loyal and steady. I knew she'd been right, but I'd simply thought I didn't want to go through the mess of being vulnerable again, of loving someone again. I *had* loved Cindy in the way that I could before the battles of life had tempered me like steel. Now, I knew what it was like to fall in love after being hurt, after betrayal, after loss, and grief. This love ran deeper. This love was wiser.

I just wondered how to get Farrah to believe in it. To believe in us.

Chapter Thirty-One

FARRAH

"Ouch!" I exclaimed. The box I'd been holding clattered to the floor, just as Tiffany walked into the supply room.

Her eyes bounced down to the box of sharps and back up to me. "Did you just stab yourself?"

I was sucking on the end of my fingertip. "No. Paper cut on the edge of the cardboard. I wasn't paying attention."

Tiffany walked toward me, leaning down to lift the box off the floor and set it on the table in the middle of the room. She headed over to the first-aid kit mounted on the wall. A moment later, she ordered me to rinse my finger in the sink.

"Paper cuts are the worst," she said as she put a small bandage on the end of my finger.

"I know. They hurt like hell, and they bleed a lot."

"Worst one I ever got was a bloody mess." She shook her head. "I was on speakerphone for a conference call and bored out of my mind. You know those calendars that cover your desk?" At my nod, she continued, "I was trying to get a paper clip out from under it so I was dragging my finger along the edge. Somehow, I managed to cut my finger on like seven pieces of paper from that damn calendar." She rolled her eyes.

"That must've hurt."

She snorted. "It did. Blood was everywhere. For the rest of the year, that calendar had blood splotches on it because it went through every freaking page." She stepped away to wash her hands in the sink. "Have you heard from your patient?" she asked over her shoulder.

"He texted. He's awake and halfway okay." I took a quick breath. "I cannot believe he just crashed in his bed. He had no food or water for like a day and a half."

"He was sick. I just hope you don't get whatever he has."

"I feel fine," I replied.

"You're going home to check on him at lunch?" she prompted.

I nodded. I'd been feeling out of sorts since I found Cooper yesterday. Or, rather, since I'd realized I was in love with him. I'd needed to put some distance between us. Then he'd gotten sick, and now I didn't know how to fix my feelings.

"Are you okay?" Tiffany stepped closer, her concerned gaze skating over my face.

I opened my mouth to insist I was perfectly okay. Instead, I hiccuped and tears stung my eyes before splashing onto my cheeks. "I'm fine," I croaked.

"Uh, clearly, you're not fine," Tiffany pointed out, her tone gentle. She guided me across the hallway to sit down in the break room. "What's going on?"

Alice appeared because it was lunchtime, and we had an actual lunch break here when we closed the office. Next thing I knew, I was telling my friends everything. Cooper and I had been foolish. I'd thought I could play it cool like I always did, but I was the opposite of cool and had gone and fallen in love with him. I didn't want to get into everything with my stepfather, so I left that messy bit alone and told them I'd always promised myself I would never fall for anyone.

"It's never been a problem. Until Cooper. He just has to go and be so nice," I explained at the end.

"Have you thought about talking to him about how you feel?" Alice asked gently.

I swiped at my tears and blew my nose with a tissue that Tiffany had handed me moments earlier. "I told him we needed space. Right before—" I waved my hand vaguely in the air. "They all went out on that trip for the fire. I missed him the whole time, and now he's sick, and I can't stop worrying about him. Ugh."

"I think you should tell him how you feel. Because no matter what, you feel what you feel. Either you put this out there, or—" Alice shrugged. "You don't. Cooper is not some jerk who will screw you over. He's a really nice guy."

I blinked away my tears, wiping my cheeks with the heels of my palms. "I know he is."

"Maybe you have to be brave," Tiffany offered.

I looked at my two friends. "You're both just saying this because you're in love," I muttered.

"So what if we are?" Alice pressed. "News flash: so are you."

———

I was nervous when I crested the top of the stairs and turned into the hallway. My eyes landed on Cooper's door before bouncing to mine. I wondered if he had gone back to his apartment. I was tiptoeing, which was ridiculous.

When I heard the muted sound of the television coming from my apartment, butterflies spun in my belly, the nervous kind. I tapped lightly on the door before I opened it, peering around to see Cooper sitting on the couch with Humpty on the cushions by his shoulders.

Cooper glanced over. "Hey there." His voice sounded a little stronger but still hoarse.

"Hey." I stepped into my apartment, closing the door behind me. After leaving my coat, shoes, and purse by the door, I approached the couch, nervously rubbing the hem of my shirt between my fingers. My heart was pounding too hard and fast. "You look a little better," I observed.

He did look better. His color was looking close to normal. He must've showered because his hair was still damp. I was so relieved to see him, so relieved he was home that I wanted to simply bask in his presence.

His eyes held mine. "I do feel better. I'm not one-hundred percent, but thanks to you, I think I'm a lot further along than I would've been if you hadn't come and gotten me. You make some seriously good chicken and dumplings by the way."

When his lips curled at the corners, my belly flipped and my heart started kicking harder. "I'm glad you had something to eat."

I rounded the loveseat to sit down in the corner opposite him. I hadn't planned this, and in all honesty, I wasn't even sure I had the courage to tell him the truth. Before I could overthink it any more than I already had, my words stumbled out. "I'm sorry I made things weird before you left, and I'm sorry I'm about to make things even weirder. I love you, and I didn't mean to. I'm not—" I shook my head quickly. "I-I... Ugh." I dropped my face into my hands, feeling heat rise in my cheeks as I took a shaky breath. I marshaled my nerves, lifting my gaze to him. I thought he might look horrified, or panicked, or I didn't even know what.

I expected just about anything but the warm understanding I saw in his eyes. With a sigh, I sagged into the cushions. I took another breath, twisting my hands together. "I..." I tried again before sputtering out.

"Can I say something?" he interjected.

Relieved, I nodded.

He held my gaze without once looking away. "I didn't plan on it, but I love you too. And, I'm not sure what that means for us, or what you want, but maybe we could try to see where this goes."

Emotions clamored inside me—joy, hope, a fierce rush of love, all of it tangled within a sense of fragility. This, this feeling, felt as fragile as a snowflake as if just drifting to the ground would break it apart.

I stared at him and blinked quickly. I was *not* going to break down in front of this man. Before I could do or say anything else, Cooper pulled me into his arms.

"Hey, come here," he said, his tone warm and comforting.

I buried my head in his chest and burst into tears. It was a big, noisy cry. Because this was all too much. I loved him, I'd had too much time of missing him, and now he was back and he was sick, and I just wanted it all to be okay.

Cooper simply held me, seeming completely at ease with my messy burst of tears.

My tears ran out quickly. It felt like a storm clearing the air, leaving it scoured clean. I took several shaky breaths, my head still buried in his chest. He smelled good. Clean and crisp, like Cooper.

I eventually scrambled up the nerve to look at him, mortified that I'd just cried like that in front of him. When I lifted my eyes to his, he didn't look horrified. He just looked a little worried, but solid and steady.

"I'm sorry!" I blurted out.

He brushed my hair away from my cheeks, smoothing it back. "There's nothing to apologize for. Can you tell me why you weren't supposed to fall in love with anyone?" he asked gently.

My chest tightened, and a familiar sense of dread twisted in my stomach. Because whenever my stepfather came up, that was how I felt. I took a slow breath, and the tension spinning inside loosened just the tiniest bit. I needed to be honest as much for myself as for him.

"Do you remember that morning at the coffee shop?" I leaned back on the couch slightly. I couldn't be too close to anyone for this conversation.

Chapter Thirty-Two

FARRAH

Cooper's eyes held mine as he nodded slowly. "Of course. I heard you say something to your mom about your stepdad throwing a cupcake against the wall on your birthday."

I cleared my throat, swallowing through the knot of pain that rose swiftly. "Yeah. Gerald was my stepfather. My father died when I was three. I don't remember him. My mom married Gerald when I was in first grade. He was nice at first, but it didn't last. He was awful. I hated him. He was mostly abusive to my mother." I took an unsteady breath, grateful that Cooper stayed quiet and patiently waited for me to explain. "When I was in college, I took a course in psychology, and they talked about domestic violence. And, I swear, it was like they were describing Gerald in the textbook. He isolated my mom from her friends and my grandparents, but it wasn't blatant. It just happened. It was just the three of us. Most of the time, he wasn't violent. It was just sometimes, just enough to keep both of us on edge and constantly wondering when he was going to explode. The day that you heard me talking about with my mom, that was the birthday when I turned ten. We didn't have a lot of money. Not because Gerald didn't have money but because he controlled it all. He was a lawyer. His whole family was lawyers, or that's what it seemed like to me. My mom worked, and all of her money went into his bank account. She had to check with him about the budget and everything. It was crazy or, at least, it felt crazy. I promised myself I would never fall in love because it wasn't worth it. Gerald was nice to my mother at first. Whenever I think back to when he first started dating her, it's hard to square with the man he really was. He would bring her flowers and stuff. He was handsome. He totally wooed her. It was a whirlwind. I don't know the exact timeframe. I'd have to ask my mom. But it felt really fast. They started dating, and then they were married within maybe a few months. We moved into his house and that was it. My mom and I had been really close before that. We haven't had the best relationship for years. We're trying right now, but it's not easy. After Gerald died, my mom's friend up here offered her the chance to come stay with her. She wanted to move. I think she wanted a fresh start because she had no friends where we were from. None at all. I decided a fresh start would be good for me too." I paused, lifting my hands and letting them fall. "So there you have it. I think my dad wasn't like Gerald, but I don't remember him. My father's parents passed away, and I didn't see them after my mom married Gerald."

I managed to recite all of this calmly, but I hadn't been able to maintain eye contact with Cooper. I finally gathered up the nerve to risk a glance in his direction. I wasn't sure how to read his expression. Careful, maybe.

"Cooper?" I prompted.

"Your stepdad was a fucking asshole," he said. I'd never seen Cooper angry, but right this second, he looked furious. His jaw was set in a hard line, and his eyes were flashing fire. Yet he was completely controlled.

I paused, mentally scanning my body. Because of Gerald and all my mother and I went through with him, anger tended to make me anxious, bordering on fearful. I held Cooper's gaze, waiting for the familiar anxiety to start churning inside. It didn't. I didn't fear him at all.

I took a shaky breath, feeling a strange sense of relief at laying out the bare truth of that part of my life. "I know he was a fucking asshole. For a long time, I was mad at my mom for not protecting us, for not leaving him. I knew he used to threaten her that he would kill her or himself if she left. I learned afterward he also threatened that he would win custody of me in court. Since he was a lawyer, and his family had money, she believed him. She felt stuck. Then he died. You know that scar you asked me about on my back?" My heart started pounding faster. I'd almost never talked about this part of the story. My mom knew, and I had once told my therapist, the one I saw after I turned eighteen. She told me if I'd been a child, she would've had to report it.

Cooper nodded very slowly.

On the heels of a deep breath, I continued, "That was one of the few times he got violent with me. I was fifteen then and was angry with him all the time. I started to talk back, and I didn't really understand how dangerous that was, not just for me, but for us, for my mom. Gerald didn't want me to do something with a friend. Everything had to go through him. He wouldn't give me the money for movie tickets. I started to argue about it, and he pushed me, really hard. I fell into a chair and a vase fell off the table beside it. I fell on my side where the glass from the vase shattered, and I had to go get stitches. I was a crying mess, and I wanted to tell the doctors what really happened, but I didn't. I told them I fell. They even brought in the police and some interviewer. I just kept saying that I fell, which was true. It's just that Gerald's the one who pushed me."

I happened to glance down and saw that Cooper's hand was curled into a tight fist on his thigh. Reflexively, I reached over, my hand landing on his forearm. "It's over. He's dead," I said.

Cooper's gaze lifted to mine. I watched as he took a slow breath, his shoulders rising with it. When he let his breath out, I could feel the tension easing in his body. "I know he's gone, but what he did is still not okay. It never will be."

I felt a surge of something inside. I didn't know how to describe it. A rush of emotion and gratitude and fierce relief. While I could still feel Cooper's anger at my stepfather, there was no sense of him being out of control. Not even a little.

"How are you and your mom now?" he asked.

I took a quick breath, letting it out with a sigh as I shrugged. "We're okay. I love her. I just didn't understand when I was younger. I thought I was being protective when I started arguing back with Gerald, but it only made it worse for her. She's never said a word to me about that, but I can see it now. It sucks that people like that can ruin lives, you know. We're just taking it a bit at a time and trying to build a better relationship. I'm glad she's safe now. She's with her friend. She's reconnected with my grandparents. She's even visiting them for the first time in a really long time."

Cooper studied me quietly, the intensity in his eyes sending my heart into a twist in my chest. "I'm so sorry." He lifted a hand to reach over and lightly trail his fingers along the side of my cheek and down over my shoulder. "I realize this might not mean anything, but I've never been violent. With anyone. I would never hurt you."

My chest felt tight, and tears stung my eyes as I held his gaze. "I know," I whispered. "I don't know how I know, but I know."

"I love you," he said solemnly. "If I could change what happened to your mom and you, I would in a heartbeat."

I blinked away my tears. "I know you would. And I love you." I swallowed and tried to lighten the moment. "Even though *that* was never supposed to happen." I leaned forward and quickly pressed a kiss to his cheek. When I leaned back, I asked, "And what about you? When this all started, I thought we were on the same page. You know? That page where neither one of us wanted romance or anything like that. I know a little bit, I know that Cindy cheated on you with your friend, but tell me the whole story."

Chapter Thirty-Three

COOPER

Farrah looked at me, her eyes warm and soft. I felt a rush of emotion. Aside from knowing that I loved her and finally coming to this point with us, telling the story seemed easy because it was her.

I summarized the whole thing—my dad dying, my parents having a really good marriage and feeling blessed, and then feeling so bitter and betrayed after what happened with Cindy.

"And I know I'm lucky," I said. "My parents had a good marriage. I was so devastated when my dad died." I shrugged. "Now, of course, Cindy feels awful about everything that happened. Things didn't work out for her and Dan, I guess." I shook my head slightly. "I imagine it doesn't feel good for her to have everybody know what happened. You can't keep a secret like that in Stolen Hearts Valley. That town is as small as Willow Brook."

Farrah nodded. "She came to visit when your mom was here, thinking maybe that would be the time to try again with you?"

"I think so. I'm still not sure why she thought there would ever be a chance."

"You didn't deserve that," Farrah said, her green eyes flashing fire.

"Nobody would've. Just like you and your mom didn't deserve the way your stepdad treated you. I don't think what I went through is even close to that."

She studied me thoughtfully. "You can't compare life experiences. Sure, violence and the trauma it leaves in its wake aren't the same as someone cheating, but that kind of betrayal—being betrayed by someone with a friend—that's next level, and not in a good way. It's different. I guess in the aftermath, we all just try to trust again."

Chapter Thirty-Four

FARRAH

One week later

Rain fell in buckets from the sky, and you couldn't dash anywhere from your car without getting drenched. The wind blew sideways, making it even more dicey out. I looked through the blurry windows of my car and steeled myself before climbing out into the deluge.

I ran as fast as I could from my car into the back door of my apartment building. Once I made it safely inside and closed the door behind me, I stopped. I was out of breath, and water dripped onto the floor. My legs were soaked. The sky had been clear with a bright sun this morning, and I hadn't realized it was supposed to rain. I ran a hand over my wet hair and laughed, resigned to my soaking-wet state. I tromped up the stairs, eyeing the water trail guiding me upward. Cooper must've just gotten home as well.

When I opened the door at the top of the stairs

into our shared hallway, I saw Cooper standing just outside our doors. He was also dripping wet.

He turned to look at me. "Hey," I said with a laugh slipping out. "You're as wet as I am."

"I was trying to decide which apartment to go into," he offered with a wry grin.

"I vote for yours. You have the washer and dryer. I'll race you to the bathroom."

It was on. We stumbled toward his door. Humpty sat on the windowsill in the hallway, and he dashed after us.

I elbowed Cooper out of the way when we got to his bathroom door. We were both laughing and breathless by then. A second later, he was kissing me and pressing me against the wall. My lips were cool from the rain. The shock of his lips on mine was a fiery contrast to the shivery cold I felt from getting drenched.

We stripped quickly, leaving our clothes in a messy scatter on the floor. We were in a rush to get our hands on each other. I was relieved we'd had the birth control conversation the other evening, and I'd let him know I was on the pill, so we no longer had to worry about condoms. Just now, I didn't want to think. I simply wanted him.

Moments later, steam was rising around us in the shower and Cooper was cupping my face with both hands as we kissed deeply. We broke free, both almost giddy at the moment as we stared at each other. I could feel his arousal against my belly.

"Hurry," I gasped.

His shower had a small seat in the corner, just a little triangle. He turned, sitting down and pulling me onto his lap. Straddling him, I let out a satisfied hum when he positioned his thick crown at my entrance. "Now," he rasped.

When I sank down over him, sheathing him inside me, I whimpered at the luscious stretch and the feel of the gliding friction.

"Look at me."

I opened my eyes, ensnared in his dark gaze instantly.

He rocked deeper into me. "I love you."

My heart clamored for joy with a thundering beat. "I love you too."

He captured my mouth again, and moments later, my release spun through me as he held me close. I flew apart with pleasure ricocheting everywhere inside.

After we actually showered, we lounged on the couch as the rain poured down outside. We ordered takeout because neither one of us wanted to go back out in that weather. Everything still felt fresh for us, but it felt good, *really* good. We fell asleep at my place that night because, as Cooper pointed out, my bed was more comfortable.

The following morning, I met my mom for coffee. She had returned from her visit with my grandparents. It felt as if she and I were gradually building something new. We had scaffolding for our relationship now. It was sturdy, but we needed to keep building. My grandparents were going to come to Alaska for a visit. I'd spoken with them on the phone several times. They were so excited, and it felt kind of strange. This part of my life had been shut off, a door closed and bolted shut by my stepfather. Now, the door was open, and I peered through it, trying to get the lay of the land. I was nervous and uncertain but relieved this pathway was now open in my life.

I looked across the table at my mother. "How was the trip?"

She was quiet for a long moment, and then she smiled with a sheen of tears in her eyes. On the heels of a breath, she nodded. "Really good. I keep saying it to you and to myself. I can't change the past, but I'm just going to hope things keep moving forward in a better way."

My heart beat unsteadily. "I'm glad, Mom. You're okay. *We* are okay."

Anxiety spun in my chest because I wanted to tell her about Cooper, but our relationship was so new. I didn't talk about relationships with her, or anyone, because there'd never been one to talk about. I finally took a breath and simply told her, ending with, "I didn't ever expect something like this. I hope it's okay."

"Can I meet him?" she asked, her tone hesitant.

Her question alone broke my heart. "Of course, Mom. I want you to meet him, and I don't see how you can't. I mean, Willow Brook is definitely a small town."

Just then, I heard the bell on the door to the café jingle, heralding the arrival of customers. I *knew* Cooper came in without even looking.

Because I had to know if my senses were spot-on, I glanced over to see him walking in with Rowan and Wes. When he saw me, he smiled, and I gestured for him to come over to our table.

"Is that Cooper?" my mom asked as he approached.

I should've been nervous, but I wasn't, not even a little. "Yeah. It's him."

EPILOGUE

Cooper

Two years later

I adjusted my shoulders. Rowan glanced over, flashing a quick grin. "Looking good. Are you ready?"

"As I'll ever be."

I was *beyond* ready. In three minutes, my wedding ceremony would start. Rowan was my best man. We'd been pretty good friends back in Stolen Hearts Valley and had gotten closer since I joined the hotshot crew here in Willow Brook.

He studied me for a moment, his gaze sobering. "I'm glad you're getting married to Farrah."

"You are?"

He nodded. "When you came out here, and I heard what had happened with Cindy, it didn't suit you to be the cynical guy. That was never your personality. When you and Cindy got engaged, it made sense at the time. Not necessarily because I thought she was the one for you, but because you're that kind of guy. Loyalty and commitment mean a lot to you, and you and Farrah are right for each other. Things usually work out the way they're supposed to. Sometimes life bangs us up a little bit before we get there."

A few hours later, I looked down at Farrah, my heart still feeling almost stunned by the day. Our reception was in full swing on the deck overlooking the lake behind Wildlands Lodge. The sun was setting, leaving a shimmer of tangerine and gold on the lake and the sky. Farrah was laughing at something Tiffany had just said. Rowan's earlier observation before the wedding echoed in my thoughts. I couldn't imagine committing my heart to anyone other than Farrah. In hindsight, I wasn't so sure it would've worked out for Cindy and me. I would've preferred to be spared the double betrayal of her and a friend. But that very betrayal was what led me to Alaska and ultimately to Farrah.

Farrah turned and glanced up at me. "What is it?" she prompted.

She'd changed out of her wedding dress. We had wanted the reception to be casual. Even though it was late summer in Alaska, the air was brisk. She was wearing a jade-green silky blouse that brought out her eyes.

"Just thinking. I love you," I replied simply.

Her eyes twinkled with her smile. "Good thing you do because now we're married. It would be a project to break up."

I chuckled. Dipping low, I slipped an arm around her waist and kissed her. Again. "When can we go home?" I asked when I straightened.

Home, for now, was Farrah's apartment, which we officially shared. Someone else had moved in across the hallway in my old place. After tonight, I had a surprise for her.

"How about now?" she suggested.

"Sounds good to me."

We said our goodbyes and slipped away. Humpty waited for us when we got home. He still liked to twine around our ankles when we came in. After that, he returned his focus to looking out the window.

We'd been together for two years now, and I didn't think a wedding ceremony would make that much difference. Since I'd felt committed by heart to Farrah ever since I'd come to terms with my feelings, I'd considered our wedding more of a formality than anything.

But somehow, my heart was in my throat and my emotions were rushing in like a high tide. I palmed her cheek, staring deep into her eyes.

"I meant every word today," I whispered gruffly.

She placed her palm over my heart, and it lunged toward her touch. My heart recognized her.

"I know you did. I love you," she whispered.

Seconds later, we were kissing and tugging at each other's clothes. Everything felt frantic until I lifted her into my arms, and we tumbled into the bed. She straddled me, her eyes on mine as she rose above and sheathed me in her silky, clenching core.

Only after we found our release could I take the time to savor her. I felt startlingly alive and at peace when she curled against me later, her fingers tracing lazy circles on my chest.

This—Farrah, us—was everything I wanted.

FARRAH

"Where *are* we going?" I pressed.

It was the morning after our wedding. Cooper's mother was in town, and my grandparents were here, and we had the logistics of family visiting to manage. We had decided to save our honeymoon for late winter when it was still cold and getting muddy, and everyone in Alaska couldn't wait for warmer days and no snow. It would be a reward to travel to Hawaii then.

For today, Cooper said he had a surprise for me.

"First, we're getting coffee," he announced.

I was going to argue against that. Moments later, Janet smiled brightly at me from across the counter. "Here's your coffee." Janet was always friendly, and I considered her family, almost like a bonus mother. When I saw the look in her eyes when she smiled at Cooper, I knew something was up.

"What is it?" I prompted, just as Beck and Maisie walked in with Rowan and Mae.

"What are you talking about?" Beck prompted.

"Janet knows something," I said with a suspicious glance in her direction.

When my eyes arced about the group, I knew that *everyone* knew something. I felt left out, and I didn't like it.

"What do you know?" I nudged Beck with my elbow where he had stopped to stand beside me.

He jumped back, chuckling as he held his palms up. "Don't ask me." He glanced toward Cooper. "You'd better get going."

Cooper winked and escorted me out to the parking lot. "How does everybody know whatever they know? Except me," I grumbled when we were in his truck.

The glow of our wedding and a night wrapped up in Cooper's arms was fading fast.

"Just wait," he said firmly.

A few minutes later, he turned down the side road, just a little bit out of the main downtown area of

Willow Brook. "Firefly Lane. This is where Graham and Madison live," I pointed out.

"Mm-hmm," he replied noncommittally.

He drove past the driveway that led to their place. After another good half mile, he turned down the next driveway. When he pulled up outside the house, I looked around. A field of fireweed at the height of its bloom grew pretty and bright pink on one side. The other side of the house was mostly spruce trees and forest with a view of the mountains rising above the trees.

"Are we having an in-town honeymoon?" I asked when we climbed out.

He reached for my hand when we met in the front of his truck, replying, "Something like that."

The house was nestled into a small rise. Two stories tall, it had a green steel roof with a modern feel to it with clean lines, dark stained wood siding and lots of windows, including a circular one in the center where the roof came to a peak on the upper floor.

Cooper led me inside before he turned to face me and reached for both of my hands. "We're home." His grip was warm and sure.

I blinked, confused. "Huh? Home?"

He palmed my cheek with one hand, his touch warm and electric at once. His gaze held mine, and my heart fluttered in my chest. Whenever Cooper looked at me like that, I felt safe, secure, and cherished, the emotional equivalent of what I'd always wanted the idea of home to be.

"Home," he repeated. "This is ours."

"What?!" My eyes went wide. "How —"

He gave me a quick and fierce kiss. Lifting his hand, he tucked a loose lock of hair behind my ear. "You said you never really felt like you had a home. I want to make sure that you always feel like you do with me. I figured the best way to do that was to get us an actual home."

I spun around, emotion rising swiftly inside as I took it in. I wanted to run around and see everything. But really, all I wanted was Cooper.

When I turned back to face him, I pressed my palm to his chest, the steady and strong beat of his heart grounding me.

"Before you worry about moving and everything right after we got married, we can take our time. But—"

I interrupted. "I want to move now! Today!"

He laughed, lifting me in his arms and spinning me around.

We moved the day after our wedding. He'd also lined up all our friends to help because he guessed I might want to move immediately. Conveniently, plenty of our friends were hotshot firefighters, all strong and sturdy. It went surprisingly fast, all things considered. I discovered that when you didn't have time to think about moving and just threw everything into boxes as fast as you could, it made the whole process much less stressful.

It was past midnight, and I stood in our new-to-me kitchen with boxes surrounding me on the floor. I smiled up at him when he set the almost empty pizza box on the counter. "What?" he prompted.

My lips curled when I walked over and stood in front of him. I must've thought I loved him hundreds of times today. "I can't believe you did this," I said softly.

I felt the curve of his smile against my lips when he kissed me. When he straightened, I added, "This is incredible, but just so you know, *you* are what's home for me."

Thank you for reading Farrah & Cooper's story! Want a glimpse of the future for them? Join my newsletter to receive an exclusive scene.

Sign up here: https://BookHip.com/JFPVMTW

p.s. If you are already subscribed, you'll still be able to access the scene.

Up next in the Fireweed Harbor Series is Be The One.

Kenan and Quinn are best friends. Just friends.
That's it.

Until one kiss. One of those earth-shaking, knee-melting, mind-blowing kisses.

Don't miss Kenan & Quinn's smokin' hot, friends to lovers, holiday romance!

Pre-order Be The One - due out Oct 9, 2023!

For more swoony romance...

This Crazy Love kicks off the Swoon Series - small town southern romance with enough heat to melt you! Jackson & Shay's story is epic - swoon-worthy & intensely emotional. Jackson just happens to be Shay's brother's best friend. He's also *seriously* easy on the eyes. Shay has a past, the kind of past she would most definitely like to forget. Past or not, Jackson is about to rock her world. Don't miss their story! Free on all retailers!

Burn For Me is a second chance romance for the ages. Sexy firefighters? Check. Rugged men? Check. Wrapped up together? Check. Brave the fire in this hot, small-town romance. Amelia & Cade were high school sweethearts & then it all fell apart. When they cross paths again, it's epic - don't miss Cade's story!
Free on all retailers!

For more small town romance, take a visit to Last Frontier Lodge in Diamond Creek. A sexy, alpha SEAL meets his match with a brainy heroine in Take Me Home. Marley is all brains & Gage is all brawn. Sparks fly when their worlds collide. Don't miss Gage & Marley's story!
Free on all retailers!

If sports romance lights your spark, check out The Play. Liam is a British footballer who falls for Olivia, his doctor. A twist of forbidden heats up this swoon-worthy & laugh-out-loud romance. Don't miss Liam & Olivia's story.
Free on all retailers!

Visit my store to purchase ebooks & fun swag!

J.H. Croix Shop

Fireweed Harbor Series

Make You Mine

Dare To Fall

Be The One - due out Oct 2023!

Light My Fire Series

Wild With You

Hold Me Now

Only Ever Us

Fall For Me

Keep Me Close

With Every Breath

All It Takes

Take Me Now

Dare With Me Series

Crash Into You

Evers & Afters

Come To Me

Back To Us

Take Me There

After We Fall

Swoon Series

This Crazy Love

Wait For Me

Break My Fall

Truly Madly Mine

Still Go Crazy

If We Dare

Steal My Heart

Into The Fire Series

Burn For Me

Slow Burn

Burn So Bad

Hot Mess

Burn So Good
Sweet Fire
Play With Fire
Melt With You
Burn For You
Crash & Burn
That Snowy Night
Brit Boys Sports Romance
The Play
Big Win
Out Of Bounds
Play Me
Naughty Wish
Diamond Creek Alaska Novels
When Love Comes
Follow Love
Love Unbroken
Love Untamed
Tumble Into Love
Christmas Nights
Last Frontier Lodge Novels
Take Me Home
Love at Last
Just This Once
Falling Fast
Stay With Me
When We Fall
Hold Me Close
Crazy For You
Just Us

ACKNOWLEDGMENTS

Here we are again: the end of the book. I often wonder who keeps on reading after the past page of the story. Alas, if you are here, thank you from thee bottom of my heart. This author thing can be immensely rewarding with the flip side of being deeply challenging. You, my readers, are why I keep writing. THANK YOU!

Thank you to my editor for helping me give Cooper & Farrah my best. Much appreciation to my proofreader who finds the funniest details I mess up. As always, hugs to my early readers who point out the errors trying to sneak through multiple rounds of editing.

Gracious thanks to Najla Qamber for making such beautiful covers for this series. Hugs & massive thanks to the bloggers, bookstagrammers, and booktokers who share their love of romance with the world.

To DBC and our dogs. All my love.

xoxo
J.H. Croix

ABOUT THE AUTHOR

USA Today Bestselling Author J. H. Croix lives in a small town with her husband and two spoiled dogs. Croix writes contemporary romance with sassy women and alpha men who aren't afraid to show some emotion. Her love for quirky small-towns and the characters that inhabit them shines through in her writing. Take a walk on the wild side of romance with her bestselling novels!

Places you can find me:
jhcroixauthor.com
jhcroix@jhcroix.com

facebook.com/jhcroix
instagram.com/jhcroix
bookbub.com/authors/j-h-croix